# The Ram of Sweetriver

He went on a little further. There was no sign of the rich lush meadows he was expecting. Instead there was a barren blackened waste of burnt stubble, now drenched like everything else by the storm. Not a blade of green grass could be detected anywhere.

Jacob stared in horror at the sight. What had happened? Where had he come to?

# The Ram of Sweetriver

Colin Dann

**RED FOX**

A Red Fox Book

Published by Random Century Children's Books
20 Vauxhall Bridge Road, London SW1V 2SA

A division of the Random Century Group

London Melbourne Sydney Auckland
Johannesburg and agencies throughout
the world

First published by Hutchinson Children's Books 1986
Beaver edition 1987
Reprinted 1988
Red Fox edition 1990
Reprinted 1991

Printed and bound in Great Britain by
Cox & Wyman Ltd, Reading, Berkshire

ISBN 0 09 951240 8

# Contents

## Dedication

For my father and mother
with all my love

# —1—
# The Flood

The rain had been falling steadily in August for nearly a fortnight. Day after day it poured down from the lowering mass of cloud that hung over Sweetriver like an immense grey sponge: it seemed the water never could be quite squeezed out. It was immovable, and the inhabitants of Sweetriver felt that their world had become one of water.

The village of Sweetriver lay on either side of the mouth of the River Leck, the two sides linked by a narrow bridge. Its streets and lanes were steep. The land rose sharply behind the promenade, and then climbed remorselessly up beyond the village, through deep valleys and gorges to the moorland and forest of the uplands. The river had its source up here. Now it rushed with increasing might down through the village towards the sea.

And there was not only the river – every rivulet and tributary was swollen. The village streets were flooded and the drains were choked; they could take no more. The gardens, too, stood under water. The surrounding fields and pastures became swamps into which the animals sank up to their knees, and even the houses began to feel damp. High up, the peaty moorland could absorb no more moisture . . . then the final catastrophe occurred.

On the night of 13 August a heavy storm broke. The rain crashed down in torrents and in an hour the moorland was awash. The river burst its banks and the storm, with incredible violence, drove the floodwater down towards the village. The farms lying higher up suffered serious damage, the animals in the fields drowned and uprooted trees crashed to the ground. The land was scoured by this furious onslaught: plants, soil, trees, rocks and boulders were swept away in the floodwater. The little bridges across the valley were smashed one by one. Telegraph poles were felled. Power cables broke and impenetrable darkness spread over the devastated countryside.

Those people who had made their homes in the valley had almost no warning of their fate. Most were in bed when the storm began and although the din had kept them awake, they had no idea how serious the situation really was. When they looked out of their windows they found they could see very little, so they did not know their houses were threatened. The worst horrors were reserved for the farmhouses and cottages lying on lower ground. These were directly in the path of the incalculable mass of water and debris which had continued to gather momentum as it descended towards the sea.

At Rookery Farm Matthew Talbot, a sheep farmer, and his wife Joan had returned late after visiting some friends in the village. As they rushed indoors out of the storm, Talbot thought he could hear a distant howl above the moaning wind. 'Sounds like Kep,' he muttered uncertainly. Kep was his sheepdog, a Welsh Collie bitch.

'Can't be,' his wife replied. 'She'll be in her kennel now.'

'I think I'll take a look anyway and get her indoors,' said Talbot. 'It's a deluge out there.'

He did not realize then how apt his words were. He

dashed outside again, and round the corner of the farmhouse to where the dog was usually kept. He found the kennel chain snapped in two, the kennel turned on its side and no sign of Kep. 'Kep! Kep! Come on, girl!' he called, and he heard the terrified beast answer with a faint whine and a howl of fear.

Talbot had no idea where she was – the noise and darkness made it impossible to tell. He continued to call, rather hopelessly, for a few minutes, while the rain drove at him mercilessly, soaking him. Then, at last, he went back indoors.

'No sign of her,' he told his wife. 'She's broken free and wandered off. I can hear something, but—'

'She'll come back on her own eventually,' his wife said, 'when the storm's abated a bit. No good worrying – you can't search for her in this.'

Kep, however, had no mind to return home. With an animal's sixth sense, she knew of the impending disaster that was descending on the house with breakneck speed, and it was this that she had been so desperate to escape.

Some minutes later, Talbot heard a roar, quite different from the other noises all around him. He stopped at the foot of the stairs, listening, as the roar grew louder. His wife faced him from the landing.

'What's that?' she whispered.

Talbot took a couple of steps up. 'I don't know . . .' he began.

The next instant the house was engulfed by the full force of the flood. The stone building, which had endured three hundred years of every kind of weather, was battered to pieces. By an extraordinary act of providence, the stairwell and part of the connecting wall and landing remained intact. The rest of the house disintegrated – but the two people survived.

Shocked and stunned beyond belief, Talbot nevertheless had the presence of mind to leap up the tottering
staircase, grab his wife and drag her down after him.
Here they huddled, cowering on the bottom step, whilst
masonry, roof timbers and tiles crashed around them
and were hurled along by the current.

Further downstream, as the floodwater galloped on
towards its outlet to the sea, some people managed to
evacuate their homes in time, knowing that they would
have no homes to return to. In Sweetriver itself, the last
remaining bridge connecting the two halves of the village
had collapsed. The village was now entirely exposed to
the mountains of water which carried tree trunks,
boulders, furniture, masonry, boats and cars with it, and
proceeded to sweep through Sweetriver and flood into
the sea.

By the time rescue teams had arrived it was too late for
many to be saved. The rescue work was hampered by the
chaos in the destroyed village and by the awful darkness
and it was hours before the Talbots were reached. They
had suffered severely from exposure and shock, and were
badly cut and bruised – but they were only two among
many in the same plight. All these people were taken for
treatment to the nearest hospital outside the area of
devastation.

A few animals escaped death, most of these purely by
chance. Amongst them was Kep, the Talbot's black and
white sheepdog. She had swum feebly, borne along at the
edge of the current, and had finally managed to pull herself out on to a tree stump. Then she had been able to
climb on to higher ground away from the boiling flood
water. Here she stood shivering, with her matted coat
dripping pools of water whilst she howled out her
misery.

Higher up the valley still, on a sort of plateau of pasture land, the Talbots' flock of sheep had miraculously survived the catastrophe intact. The waters had thundered all around this plateau but had descended either side of it, so that the frightened sheep stood in a sodden field, their fleeces pouring rivers of rainwater, but otherwise unscathed.

By first light the northerly wind had dropped and the rain lessened to a drizzle. Eventually, the storm clouds shifted in a new breeze and began to move away slowly from Sweetriver, having wrought their havoc and caused a state of emergency to be declared in the county.

# — 2 —
# The Ram of Sweetriver

The Talbots' sheep were the only sheep in the area of Sweetriver, principally one of dairy farming, so they had come to be known as the Sweetriver flock. They were hill sheep: hardy animals with dense fleeces, stocky and rather chubby in appearance, with white faces and rudimentary horns. The flock consisted of about forty breeding ewes and their twenty-five lambs, recently weaned. There were some barren ewes amongst them and these were fatter than the others. There was also one ram in the flock. He was getting old and coming to the end of his breeding life. He, alone of the rams, had been allowed to run with the flock so that he might fatten up during the summer on good pasture. And he, alone of the rams, survived. The other mature males, in their separate area, all fell victim to the flood and were drowned. This surviving ram was a very wise beast, experienced in the ways of predators and with a knowledge of all sorts of dangers. He was called Jacob.

Jacob was still a fine, strong-looking beast; his face had a noble expression and he had the massive curling horns of the male. He looked confident and content and most of the time he was of an easy-going temperament. In his day he had mated with many of the ewes, but his favourite was Myriam. She was the eldest ewe and of a placid and motherly disposition. Barley, another ewe in the flock, was openly scornful of Myriam, who tended to ignore her. She had a rather frivolous nature and cared little for Jacob's authority. Then there was Bell, a pretty little ewe, with a very serene appearance. She admired Jacob enormously and was jealous of all the females to whom he showed any attention.

Some of the lambs were daughters and sons of Jacob, the progeny of what was intended to be his final tupping season. Frolic was Jacob's favourite daughter; loveable and loyal. Of his sons, Reuben was the biggest; a strong lamb who already showed signs of independence. Myriam was the mother of these two lambs. Jacob was also father to Jess, who had a less strong character and seemed only to want to imitate his father, following him closely whenever he could.

For some time now Jacob had been warning the flock to expect bad weather. He had sensed the storm's approach but even he had not anticipated its full fury. 'Prepare yourselves,' he had said, 'and keep together. We shall need each other's comfort soon.'

The lambs had not understood his meaning and had looked at their mothers uncertainly. But Jacob had kept his warning in their minds by murmuring from time to time: 'There's rough weather about, I know it. Yes, I know it.'

The ewes heeded him. As the clouds darkened overhead they roamed the pasture in a close-knit group, keeping their lambs next to them. Their pasture was well drained but the days of rain had made the ground softer and muddier. On the night of the storm, although the flood bypassed them their feeding ground soon became a morass. For hours in the darkness they stood shoulder to shoulder beneath the blast, trying to protect their young from harm. Jacob knew they must find shelter.

One tributary that skirted their little plateau had on its

far bank a thick brake of stunted thorn, whose twisted branches formed a dense screen. Jacob knew that was the place they should try to reach. He stood and stared at the perilous water, trying to assess its depth and flow. He knew the lambs could never swim it, even if the adult animals should be strong enough. He left the flock behind and went further upstream, lowering his heavy head against the vicious wind. All the time he searched for a crossing point.

He saw there was only one possibility. A fallen tree had wedged itself across the stream and, at every moment, threatened to be torn loose by the angry water or the buffets of the wind. But Jacob could see that, if he hurried the flock onwards, they might mount the trunk and run across in time. He returned and quickly gathered the sheep together, telling them of his plan. 'I'll go first in case of danger,' he said. 'If it's safe you must come at once, but don't rush together or jostle. Think of your lambs.'

He led them at a run to where the tree still wavered in the watercourse. With a little jump he was on it and, despite its rocking, with the surefootedness of his kind he kept his balance and trotted across. Myriam followed him. Then her young and the other ewes with their lambs followed her. Jacob watched patiently, trying to mask his fears as slowly but surely the line of sheep stepped across, leaving an ever-dwindling group on the other side.

Suddenly the tree received a particularly strong gust of wind at one end where its exposed roots were frantically flailing the water. It was nearly wrenched free but somehow the knotted roots held it back. One of the last ewes, an unmated animal, was just jumping on to the trunk as this happened. She was thrown off her feet and fell into the torrent where she was rushed downstream in an

instant. Her terrified bleats were soon lost in the noise of
the storm and in a few moments the current had dragged
her under. The remaining sheep hesitated now, looking
nervously across at their companions.

'Come on, come on,' Jacob called authoritatively.
'Soon it will be too late!'

The tree had steadied again and the rest of the
unmated females now hurried across with the utmost
haste. Immediately the last one was safe Jacob led them
all at a run to the stand of blackthorn. Ignoring the thorns
which could not pierce their thick fleeces, the flock got
right in amongst the lowest branches, glad of any relief
from the tempest which still raged across the countryside. Even as they took shelter they saw the very tree trunk
which had served them so well go crashing past them on
the spate. Its resistance to the storm had been overcome.

'Oh! Oh!' bleated Bell. 'Look at that! Jacob's so wise.
How could he have known that it was safe to cross?'

'He didn't know,' retorted Barley. 'We might all have
been washed away!'

Jacob looked on impassively. It was pointless to
remind her that they had not all been on the crossing at
once – the fact was that they were safe. But they were
reminded of the one member of the flock who had fallen
victim to the flood and some of the lambs began to ask
their mothers what had happened to her.

'She has gone,' said Myriam, answering for each. 'We
won't see her any more.'

The lambs accepted this at once. They really were not
sufficiently interested to question further and they
nestled closer to their mothers, content to be sheltered
from the storm. Some of the flock lay down where they
could to make themselves comfortable. Others nibbled
at the few tufts of herbage that sprouted under the thicket.
All the animals were tired.

Gradually a little light penetrated the massed clouds and the moaning wind dropped to a whisper. As it grew lighter the sheep could see that most of the land was under water. Jacob realized that the water was spreading and that they must move if they were not to starve. He knew that this meant climbing to higher ground but he waited a little longer before he roused the flock.

The storm had abated. Now another survivor was making her way up the valley through the drizzle. The sheepdog Kep, still soaked to the skin, had recovered her senses in the quiet of the early morning. She still would not return to the scene of her master's shattered home. Her instinct told her things were not as they had been. But she remembered her duty to prevent the flock from straying and she sensed that the sheep had moved. She knew she must act on her own.

By climbing here, paddling and swimming a little there, she reached the plateau where the flock had been pastured. Kep soon spotted the white fleeces dotted amongst the greenery on the opposite bank. She surveyed the foaming waters of the Leck's tributary that separated her from them and knew she could not swim across.

The sheep sensed Kep's presence before they saw her. A stir of awareness spread through the whole flock and they shifted nervously. Jacob moved out from the thorn screen to look. He saw the collie bitch standing on the edge of the pasture close to where the sheep had crossed during the night. He saw her matted coat, the white hairs of which were now a muddy brown. He saw her heaving sides, her long muzzle, her lolling tongue and the fixed stare she used to control the ewes. For a while the two beasts eyed one another with an even gaze. Then Jacob turned and Kep watched the ram's solid shape return unhurriedly to the thicket. With the water as a barrier,

Jacob thought the collie presented no threat.

'It's time to move on,' he said, rousing the flock. 'There are some fields higher up with good feed where I was once allowed to roam. We must go there now before we're swamped.'

'What about Kep?' Myriam asked quietly. They could all see the bitch now, hovering close.

'She'll be no problem,' Jacob said confidently, 'as long as we stay on this side.'

He moved ahead of the flock with his stately walk, splashing through the mire and pools of water. The ewes and lambs followed him. Jacob kept them well away from the bank of the stream but always in view of Kep.

The dog kept abreast of their progress, loping up and down the far bank and moving along with them. Every now and then she took a step or two down towards the water as if in two minds whether to hazard a crossing, but always she jumped back up again. 'You won't stray too far,' she yelped at the sheep in warning. 'I'll prevent you.'

The flock scurried a little off course as they heard her, but Jacob brought them back in line. 'Empty words,' he told them. 'She can't enter the flood.'

But the ewes remained unsettled and bleated amongst themselves. They knew Kep of old and were daunted by her.

The land began to rise more steeply and became firmer. Jacob was encouraged by this as he knew the danger to sheep's feet from soggy fields. Now he led the flock away from the rushing stream towards the higher levels. Kep, frustrated, started to bark.

'She'll catch us. I'm sure she'll catch us,' Bell wailed, shaking her soft, pretty head.

Kep's barks were angry and shrill: they sounded

threatening. In spite of the collie's distance, the ewes
became panicky and started to run.

'Keep behind me!' Jacob called to them. 'You don't
know the way.'

The flock quietened but the barking went on –
gradually growing fainter as they moved on.

'Of, I know she won't let us get away,' Bell continued
tremulously. 'She'll reach us somehow.'

'Be quiet, Bell!' Jacob said angrily. 'Can't you see
you're affecting the others?'

Bell was silenced: Jacob's authority was, for her,
supreme. The flock continued to climb.

Kep was furious at the flock's escape – she could see
them in the distance ascending the slope and every step
took them further away from where they ought to be. She
ran along the length of the tributary, trying in vain to find
a way of gaining access to the other bank. She knew that if
she did not stop them soon they would be lost to her
master: she ran faster.

The drizzle stopped. A warm, westerly breeze sprang
up and, at last, the clouds began slowly to disperse. Kep
watched the stream. It was still in spate but its pace had
slackened. The flood from the water table on the high
levels was gradually draining away.

Further upstream the dog finally found a crossing
place. It was like a bridge over the tributary. Here, men
had dug a channel under the turf to carry the usually
docile current, and to provide themselves and their
animals with a sort of causeway over the stream. Of
course the torrent of water from the storm had flooded
over this spot, but its depth was insufficient to prevent
Kep from swimming across, most of the current roaring
through the channel underneath. The bitch soon
reached the other side and pulling herself out, shook the
drips from her coat in a fine spray. Now she had to make up

for lost time, and she raced after the flock to cut it off.

As Kep closed the gap she could see where the sheep were heading. Instead of following them directly, she ran swiftly round in an arc to a point ahead where she could forestall them. She was a fleet-footed young collie and when Jacob's head appeared above the next rise, he saw Kep waiting for them. He halted.

Jess, who was right behind him, said: 'Is this where we stop?'

Jacob was thinking hard.

'Do we stay here now?' Jess persisted and the other animals milled about uncertainly.

'We'll have a short rest,' said Jacob quickly, trying to find time to decide what to do.

The ewes and lambs took the opportunity to graze a little, but Jacob did not feed. Kep was lying immobile, her head resting on the ground. She watched him intently, looking alert and determined. Jacob turned on his heel and descended a few paces. The rest of the flock had not climbed as high as he and could not see Kep lying in wait. Even so, Bell's doubts had infected them with unease and they were fidgety, raising their heads sharply as they grazed and staring down to the land below them for a sight of the familiar black and white body.

Jacob knew he had to deal with Kep now. If he did not, she would drive the flock downhill again to the pasture they had left and keep them there until her master returned. He wondered what he could do, wishing he could consult another member of the flock. But he dared not risk a panic by mentioning Kep's nearness. How had she reached them? Oh, she was a clever beast!

He decided he would go on alone. First he went to Myriam, the ewe he trusted the most. She was grazing by herself.

'Will you keep the flock together?' he asked her.

'They'll follow you as the eldest. There's a difficulty ahead and I have to go and see about it.'

Myriam looked at him with her soft steady eyes. She chewed her mouthful pensively, half understanding him. 'Is there some danger?' she murmured.

'There might be,' Jacob answered. 'If you hear anything, don't move for a while. Stay here. But if I don't come back lead the flock on upwards. You'll find the pasture I mentioned beyond a line of dark trees.'

'I'll do as you say,' she answered him. 'But don't risk danger, Jacob. We need you with us.'

'I'm a cautious animal,' he said simply. He gave Myriam an affectionate look and turned away. She watched him disappear over the ridge.

Jacob intended to ignore Kep and go on past her. He thought he might draw her away from her vantage point.

Kep saw Jacob coming and flattened herself against the ground. She was absolutely motionless. As soon as the flock appeared she meant to dash out and intercept them; then drive them down. But the flock did not appear. Jacob came on alone, drew level with Kep and passed by without so much as a glance. Kep lifted her head and looked at him.

She raised herself. 'Where are you going?' she called. 'You can't take the sheep up there. It's not my master's domain.'

Jacob stopped and turned. 'As you see, I'm alone,' he answered evenly. He looked at the dog without fear.

Kep looked back. She had never seen Jacob at such close quarters before. She noted his broad, strong head with the great curling horns, his muscular neck and shoulders, his firm stocky body: his whole demeanour spelt authority. She knew that, in a tussle, he would be more than a match for her. But her sense of duty and loyalty to her master were paramount.

'The others will follow you,' she muttered.

'Not until I tell them to,' Jacob returned.

'Then where are you going?' Kep repeated.

'That rather depends on you,' said the ram.

Kep licked her chops perplexedly. What would her master wish her to do with Jacob? Not lose him, at any event. The ram continued to regard her patiently.

Kep played for time. 'Why did you leave your pasture?' she questioned.

'Look behind you,' Jacob told her. 'The land is under water. How could we feed?'

'I don't have to look,' answered Kep. 'I know what happened in the night; I broke free and escaped. My master and mistress didn't but I know they're alive.'

'Then why don't you look for them?'

'If I did, you would stray, quite out of reach, and I can't allow that. That's why I'm here; it's what I've been trained for.'

Jacob admired loyalty. He could almost sympathize with the sheepdog's point of view. 'Then what do you propose?' he asked quietly.

'I propose to take the flock back to my master's land,' replied Kep.

'If you do they will all die,' Jacob warned her. 'And I can't allow that.'

There was no mistaking the challenge in the voice of the ram. Kep swallowed and began to pant.

'All right,' she said finally. 'If I let you remain here until my master comes back for you, do you agree not to wander further?'

Jacob was scornful. 'Despite your training, you don't understand sheep. We seek the best herbage. There is no good grazing here, so we must move on to find it.'

'You want to have it all your own way,' Kep yapped

angrily. 'I've tried to be reasonable.'

'That may be,' said Jacob. 'But I have to think of the well-being of the flock. How do I know when or if the master will return?'

'A good farmer looks after his animals,' Kep answered.

'Very well,' said Jacob. 'If he's as good as you believe he is, he won't want to leave us untended for long. Now listen.' He drew himself up impressively. 'I promise that the flock will stay here one day and one night. You bring the master to us. If you don't return with him by then, we will move on.'

Kep narrowed her brown eyes. 'How do I know you mean what you say?' she demanded.

'I'll keep my word.' Jacob replied, with a note of pride in his voice. 'But mind what I say. One day and one night. Is it a bargain?'

'I suppose it must be,' muttered Kep unhappily. She felt she had got the worst of this encounter.

Jacob turned and went back down the valley to the flock. He was pleased with the arrangement. He had no expectation of the farmer, nor any of his men, coming so soon after the deluge to look for them. The bargain was weighted in his favour. By the next day the flock would be up on the high pastures that he remembered from his youth.

# —3—
# To Pastures New

It was still early morning when Jacob returned to the flock. Myriam had been watching for him.

'I'm glad you're back safely,' she said to him. 'But there's some bad news. One of the young ewes – Sheba – is sick. I think she's been nibbling bracken.'

'I was afraid of something like this,' Jacob muttered. 'A lot of them are not yet wise about plants.' He looked around for the youngster. He could see the lamb lying on her side, her breathing seemed to be laboured.

'Is the danger averted?' Myriam asked.

'Yes – at least for the time being.'

'Then we should be moving?'

Jacob hesitated. He still preferred not to mention the threat from Kep. 'I think we should wait a little to see if Sheba recovers,' he said. 'She can't be moved at present. Another day will settle it one way or the other. In the meantime I must caution them all about their eating.'

'I've already done so,' Myriam told him. 'But I might have left it a little too late.'

'Perhaps they should learn the hard way,' Jacob replied. 'If Sheba dies they'll take her death to heart.'

They moved over to look at the suffering lamb. Her soft innocent eyes gazed at them piteously – she was certainly in great distress. Her breath came in short gasps and she was unable to find her voice.

'Poor thing, poor thing,' murmured Myriam compassionately.

'Don't despair,' said Jacob. 'If she only nibbled at the fern she might be sick for a while but will be on her feet again soon.'

Sheba's hopeless expression countered the ram's optimism. She alone knew how much of the plant she had swallowed.

'We can only wait,' Jacob said. 'Nothing else to be done.' He looked down the valley, his strong, broad head moving slowly round as his eyes ranged the land for a glimpse of Kep's progress. He thought he saw her, already a long way back on her return journey to the farm. But the movement he saw was just a dot on the landscape. It could have been a distant bird.

Certainly Kep had lost no time in retracing her steps. She was relieved to be free for a time from her duties with the flock. She longed to discover where her master had gone and to be reunited with him. Moreover, she was feeling hungry and she had some hopes that she might find some food amongst the ruins of her master's home.

Where she was not impeded by any sort of barrier she ran as swiftly as she ever had before. Sometimes she jumped a trickle of floodwater; sometimes she faced a wider, faster stream and was just able to swim across. But as she descended towards the farm the flooded land became more and more difficult to negotiate. She felt she was close to home, but the altered appearance of the countryside puzzled her. No landmarks remained to confirm her instincts. No human beings, no animals were visible anywhere around. Kep had a ghastly sense of being completely alone and for a moment she regretted leaving even the dubious companionship of the flock – but still she pressed on where she could. She remained

absolutely convinced that her master and mistress had
survived, and she knew, quite definitely, that sooner or
later her master would come for her.

In the end the vast expanse of water was too much for
the dog and she was prevented from proceeding further.
She sat on a piece of debris and stared disconsolately at
the receding water. She was marooned not only by the
water, but by her isolation in an empty countryside.

Kep's hunger reasserted itself. There was nothing to
eat anywhere. How long before her master would
remember her needs? She sat on, waiting patiently.

The skies had cleared by the afternoon and the August
sun shone upon the scene of devastation. On the higher
land the Sweetriver flock, under Jacob's guidance, bided
their time. Like Kep, they saw no other creatures save
birds. But the sheep were tense: they knew that one of
their number was dying.

Sheba had not moved her position all day – indeed,
she could not move. She felt too weak; too ill. Her
stomach felt as if it was on fire, yet she could tell none of
her companions about it. Her breathing was agonizingly
difficult because of the pain and she was desperate for
water.

The other lambs kept away from her, frightened by her
appearance. They did not understand what had happened to her.

Jess kept close to his father. 'Why doesn't she get up?
Why is she so still?' he kept asking.

'Jess, I've told you many times,' Jacob said wearily.
'Sheba is ill. She ate a bad plant by mistake. She's
very weak.'

'What will happen?' he persisted.

'I don't know yet. But we'll know soon enough.'

'I fear the worst,' Myriam said to Jacob later.

'Yes. It seems inevitable,' he admitted.

When dusk fell Sheba no longer felt thirsty – she was beyond any such feeling. Her pathetic young body lay quite still, unmarked by any outward sign of her suffering; a victim of her own innocence. The dead lamb's mother was silent. But another ewe, Barley, came up to Jacob.

'If we had stayed in our pasture she would still be alive,' she said to him scornfully.

'Perhaps,' said Jacob. 'But we would all soon have been cut off by the water – unable to feed.'

Barley tossed her head.

'I did the best I could for the whole flock by bringing you up here,' Jacob went on.

'Oh great wise Jacob,' the ewe bleated derisively, 'what should we do next? Will the all-knowing one speak?'

'Your sarcasm is wasted on me,' Jacob told her, turning on his heel in contempt and leaving Barley feeling a little foolish. She was angry with him for slighting her and determined to get even when she could.

The sheep passed the night peacefully enough, drowsing off and on. At dawn Jacob roused them. With the first of the light his pact with Kep ended and, as he had expected, the bitch had failed to find her master so quickly. He led them uphill again, leaving Sheba's body behind as evidence of their need to move on to sweeter grazing. Soon the carrion eaters would be gathering.

Jacob wanted to get the flock up to his old feeding ground as quickly as possible, in case Kep should return to bar their way again. But the lambs were becoming difficult; they thought they were on some sort of adventure and were excitable and frisky. Two of the male lambs, Dancer and his twin brother Prancer, went skipping away from the main flock, chasing each other about and ignoring the calls of the adults to keep together.

'I'm faster, I'm faster,' cried Dancer, running and

jumping in delight over the soaked vegetation which sparkled in the sunshine. Prancer ran after him, anxious to show off his speed to the grown-up sheep.

Their mother, a large ewe called Becky, was admonished by Jacob for not exerting proper control.

'I've called them and called them,' replied Becky, secretly proud of their antics. 'They're in such high spirits, aren't they? But it's natural, really, at their age – a sort of release from the frights we've had.'

Jacob said nothing. He thought ewes were always too self-indulgent towards their offspring. But Bridget, one of the barren females, spoke up. She was a fat sheep who seemed never to be without a mouthful of cud to chew.

'I'd call them all right if they were mine,' she declared. 'How can you let them leap about like that, holding everyone up?'

'Well, they're not yours, are they?' Becky snapped back. 'Though no doubt you'd love them to be.'

'No. It's not always the fittest to become mothers that do so,' Bridget countered bitterly.

'Stop bickering,' said Jacob. 'You're both as bad as each other.' He had no time for petty jealousies about motherhood. 'Dancer! Prancer!' he bellowed. 'Do as you're told and come back immediately!'

The lambs heard the command and trotted meekly back.

'There will be plenty of time for play later,' Jacob said to them, less severely. 'We have to reach the new pasture as soon as we can. Do you understand?'

'Yes, Jacob,' they bleated.

'The Great Ram has spoken,' Barley muttered to herself.

A little later Jacob stopped in order to get his bearings. He was searching for the line of dark trees which, he recalled, bordered the pastures they were heading for. He looked along the horizon, but recognized nothing.

'Hm . . . must be farther than I thought,' he murmured.

'Here's a thing. Jacob's lost,' chanted Barley, who was within earshot.

'I am not lost,' he answered quickly. 'I know this is the right direction.'

Barley had not expected her remark to be overheard. She tried to feign indifference.

The sheep continued with Jacob some way ahead still looking out for a clue. He did not know that, since his young days, the fields he remembered had changed ownership in a sale of land and the trees had been felled to enlarge the area for cultivation. As time went on the ram began to lose a little confidence. He dared not show it, however.

Myriam suspected that something was wrong. She knew Jacob better than any of them, and she could tell that his movements were beoming less purposeful. She hastened forward, nudging Jess to the rear.

'What is it?' she asked softly. 'Was Barley not so wrong after all?'

'It's strange, Myriam,' Jacob answered her. 'I could have sworn I knew the way. And yet, now the place seems different.'

'Well, what does that mean for us all, I wonder?' Myriam mused. 'Where will we go?'.

'I haven't given up yet,' Jacob assured her. 'We can go on a little further. There are one or two things that are familiar – that solitary rock for instance. Do you see it?'

'Yes.'

'I'm almost sure I used to look down on that from the high pastures, although of course we're below it at present. I can't be absolutely sure that I'm right.'

Now the mother of the dead lamb, Sheba, spoke out, her voice quivering with grief. 'I don't know why we keep moving like this. No animal cares about my poor baby who suffered so much. She's left to wait for the crows to pick at her. Where are we going? Why did we leave our home? I feel so wretched.'

Becky tried to comfort her. 'It must seem heartless to you,' she said. 'But what was there to be done? She is beyond help now and if we had stayed there others might have suffered the same fate. Jacob is taking us to a better place.'

The grieving ewe, Martha, looked towards Jacob and Myriam. 'He seems to be in doubt where he's taking us now,' she said miserably. 'We were in no danger on our pasture – the rain stopped eventually.'

Bell chipped in. 'You have a short memory, Martha. We left just in time. There was no pasture left – just water. But I suppose your wits have become numbed with grief.'

'Poor Martha,' murmured Frolic. 'Need you be so spiteful, Bell?'

Reuben joined them. 'Jacob thinks he's still a leader . . .' he said, 'but I think he's lost himself. Look at him, turning about this way and that. He's really too old and his memory is going. We don't have to follow him, you know.'

The ewes were speechless for a moment. What audacity from a mere lamb, big as he was!

Bell found her tongue first. 'I'm glad he didn't hear that, Reuben, for your sake. Otherwise you would soon have discovered that he's far from past it! He is our leader and we need to remember that if we're to survive. As for you . . .' she added witheringly, 'you're scarcely weaned!'

Reuben was silenced; but he was undismayed.

Presently Myriam rejoined the flock. 'The landscape has altered since Jacob came this way before,' she told them. 'He is going on ahead for a while to make sure of things. We can stay around here – there's herbage and pools to drink from.' She raised her voice. 'You youngsters! Don't be tempted by other plants – eat only what you know is safe.' Myriam wheezed a little for she was not young. Dancer and Prancer giggled and Bell echoed the sound in a titter: she was jealous of Myriam as Jacob's confidante.

The sun shone with real strength now, drying the saturated countryside. It was past noon and Jacob climbed closer to the lone rock, his sturdy body moving with deliberation. He wanted to get beyond it, higher up, to where he thought he had stood before, many years ago. Once he turned, to be sure he was not being followed by Jess or any of the lambs. He saw that the whole flock was grazing. His pace quickened: if things were not as he had supposed up ahead he did not want any of the flock to see his mistake.

After a while he reached a point where the ground levelled out. The rock was now below him and he felt almost afraid to look back at it. But he made himself, and he knew at once that he had not been wrong. From where he stood the exact shape of this chunk of stone stirred a chord in his memory that was unmistakable. Yes, he had been up here before. But the pastures – where were they? He turned back to look once more at the ground ahead. There were none here!

He went on a little further. There was no sign of the rich lush meadows he was expecting. Instead there was a barren blackened waste of burnt stubble, now drenched like everything else by the storm. Not a blade of green grass could be detected anywhere.

Jacob stared in horror at the sight. What had

happened? Where had he come to?

He walked on, blackening his feet with the grime of the wet ash and trying to turn a blind eye to this new scene of destruction. It seemed never ending. Jacob looked about for some other spark of life to comfort himself: but no bird flew or sang over this area; no living thing that had survived this firing of the land would return to the scene for quite a while. There was just an expanse of mushy blackness to look upon – and Jacob felt like an outcast as he plodded through it.

He turned in another direction, perhaps the green fields were over that way? No . . . nor this way. Soon Jacob knew that he was not going to find the pastures. Yet something made him carry on, fruitlessly searching. He dreaded returning to the flock he had led up here with the dire news that there was nothing to eat.

Dusk had begun falling before he turned once more in the direction of the solitary rock. His heart had sunk to his belly. What could he tell the sheep? That he had brought them here to no purpose? He knew that some of them would say that he was ancient and already living only in his dreams. His once proud head dropped and hung on his chest.

Footsore, grimy and dispirited, the ram of Sweetriver returned to the flock. Suddenly he heard two fierce barks. Then there was a noise like low thunder: Kep had returned and the sheep were running. Now he himself broke into a run downhill towards the flock.

He saw the flock scattering, panicking, running this way and that as Kep, her fangs bared and her tongue lolling, raced amongst them, barking constantly. She had lost all sense of training and duty. There was no man with her and it was quite obvious that she was furious.

Jacob tried to stop the terrified ewes and lambs, crying 'Stop!' over and over. But they could neither hear nor

listen. Now his anger, too, was kindled. He came briefly
to a halt and watched which way Kep was running; then
he lowered his head so that his horns faced squarely for-
wards and charged directly towards the collie.

The heavy thud of his feet on the turf was recognizable
above the noise of the other animals. Kep glanced back
and saw the huge power of the ram almost upon her. She
leapt aside. Jacob's head, with its mass of solid bone and
horn, missed her by a fraction. She flinched and her black
and white body cowered on the ground, her fury
dissipated.

Jacob halted and stamped on the turf, swinging his
head menacingly. 'What have you come back here for?'
he demanded. 'To wreak your vengeance on helpless
lambs?'

'You tricked me,' Kep called to him nervously. 'You
broke your promise.'

Jacob stared at the bitch. 'I broke a promise?' he
boomed. 'It's you who have done so. We waited where we
were but you didn't return with the man. One of our
youngsters died because of it and you dare to say—'

'I – I'm just saying this,' Kep broke in quickly. She
could see his brows were knitting and she knew what that
might mean. 'I'm saying that you promised me one day
and one night. Well, the day is not yet over and already
you've moved this far.'

Jacob congratulated himself on his foresight – he had
known there was room for ambiguity in his words. He
had intended it, to give the flock a start. He looked
around him before he replied to the dog's accusation.
Most of the sheep had already calmed down at the sight
of him. He called to the others, telling them they had
nothing to fear. Then he turned again to Kep.

'It seems you misconstrued what I said,' he remarked
in a sardonic tone. 'When I made the bargain with you

the day had barely begun. That was the day I referred to. So, once the night had passed, we moved on.'

'Cheat,' Kep growled at him. But she knew now she was beaten. 'You intended me to fall for your trick.'

Jacob did not deny it. 'Say what you like,' he answered, 'but you cannot say I didn't stick to my word. And what about your word?' he added suddenly.

'Well?' the collie growled.

'You thought this day was the day in question – yet you're here before it's over!'

'I came as dusk fell,' Kep said sullenly, 'and also because—' she broke off, licking her chops.

'Because what?'

'It doesn't matter,' she said meekly. 'You've won anyway, I won't humiliate myself as well.' She had been on the point of saying that she had felt lonely.

Jacob looked at her without animosity. At last he said: 'So you didn't find the master?'

'No.'

'I'm sorry,' said Jacob. And he meant it. 'You must be hungry.' Kep was still licking her lips.

She swallowed hard. 'I am.'

'I believe he will come for you,' Jacob said encouragingly. 'You were his favourite I think.' Then he recalled the wilderness ahead: 'We're both in difficulties,' he murmured.

But Kep did not hear the last remark. She had decided not to prolong the scene of her defeat and was already slinking away.

# —4—
# A Coming of Age

The sheepdog was soon lost from sight and Jacob was
confident that the flock would not see her again. But the
damage had been done. Some of the more nervous sheep
had run far away from Kep's angry barks. Some had even
run blindly back down the valley until their fright subsided. Myriam was quick to point this out.

'Yes, I can see a few animals below there,' Jacob said
and sighed.

'The flock's been broken up,' Myriam said.

'But why don't they come back now, silly creatures?'
Jacob cried in exasperation. 'Have we lost many?'

'It's hard to tell, but I don't think so,' Myriam
answered. She was itching to know what Jacob had found
up ahead. 'Did you find—' she began, but her question
was lost in the excited bleats of Bell and Jess, who came
gambolling around Jacob, calling him their hero.

'You were magnificent,' the ewe enthused with shining
eyes. 'That horrible dog was really daunted by you!' She
skipped round the ram in her delight.

'Jacob, please, will you teach me?' Jess implored him.
'Teach me everything you know? I want to be just like
you when I'm grown up – strong and masterful and –
and—'

'All right, all right,' Jacob said with amusement. He
was flattered despite himself. 'Calm down now. I only

did what was necessary. But you see, Bell, Kep thought she was doing what she ought to do, too. So really—'

'Horrible dog, horrible dog,' chanted Jess, aping the ewe's words.

'That will do, Jess,' Jacob said quietly. 'Kep has gone and we have other things to think about.'

Myriam looked at him sharply, expecting news. But Jacob only said, 'I must feed. My insides feel like a void. Myriam, keep the animals together in the meantime. Perhaps the stragglers will return. We'll talk later.' He knew she was waiting on his words, but he just could not bring himself to describe his alarming discovery. He needed to reflect a little on the flock's new situation. He walked a little way off and began cropping the turf greedily.

While he chewed he looked around at the ewes and lambs who now depended so much on him. Their fleeces looked clean and dry after some hours of sunshine. They looked well fed and healthy. But they could not remain where they were and, since the pastures to which they had been expecting to move had disappeared, what was to become of them? What was he to do? The more he thought about it, the more he came to accept that there was only one solution to the problem. He would have to lead them beyond the burnt fields, on and upward again until they had reached whatever lay on the highest land.

During his life Jacob had heard rumours and stories about what was up there – how there were masses of great trees in one area and open wild country in another. He had heard of the wild ponies and the other wild and, often, dangerous creatures who lived there. And he had heard how humans were not often seen there or, if they ever were, it was easy for those creatures who wished to avoid them to do so. Yes, that was where they must go: to the high land. There might be dangers ahead of them, but they must take their chance. There was no going back now, for behind them lay only desolation.

When Jacob had eased his hunger, he called Myriam to him. 'You must be the first to know,' he told her. 'I value you as no other animal and I need your support. There are no pastures above the solitary rock; even the trees I remembered have gone. There is nothing to eat, not one green shoot. It's not even fit to walk across.' Jacob looked down at his begrimed feet and hocks. 'But walk across it we must,' he added.

Myriam was looking at him in consternation; almost in fear. 'Why do we have to cross it?' she whispered.

'We have no choice, Myriam. We have to go on if we're to survive. We should soon exhaust the turf in this small area and behind us, down the valley, there is nothing but water. Even Kep can find nothing to eat. We must search higher up still for new feeding grounds.'

'And if we don't find them?'

'We will find them. I will see to it,' Jacob answered.

Myriam's look of concern vanished, dissipated by the ram's determination. This had always been the way with them; they had real faith in each other. She returned his steady, even gaze, feeling the warmth of his presence and a pride in herself that she was still his favourite ewe. How resolute and dependable he had always seemed to her. She need question him no further.

'I must warn the others,' she said.

'No, I'll do it. It's my responsibility – I brought the flock up here.'

Jacob called to the other sheep to gather together and they bunched around him. Jess got as close to his father as he could. He imitated the ram's stance and the set of his head and shoulders: he imagined himself to be another Jacob in miniature. Reuben, the big lamb, stood a little aside, looking at the ram expectantly. He was sure he had an admission of failure to give them and he was eager to see how Jacob would get round it.

Jacob began simply. 'The pastures I told you about no longer exist. I found a big change in the look of the land, and the fields where I remembered feeding have disappeared.'

The ewes started bleating all at once in dismay. The lambs looked at their mothers and were frightened. Only Reuben muttered to no animal in particular, 'A fine leader, this.'

Jacob allowed the noise to die down of its own accord. Then he said, 'Don't be alarmed, we can continue our climb now. We're free to go where we choose. There's no dog to worry us any more; Kep won't be back. Now we've all eaten our fill I'll lead you on to the land at the top of the valley.'

There seemed to be no dissent. Jacob knew the ewes well and he knew that most of them would be happy to follow his decision. 'First of all,' he went on, 'we have to cross an expanse of black burnt stubble. The quicker we get across that the better, because there can be no more grazing until we do. Have you all drunk? And are you ready to move?'

About half a dozen animals were still thirsty, so the rest of the flock waited whilst they drank from the nearest pool. Jacob looked around to see if any of the stragglers were still far away, but they had all returned to the greater safety they found in the midst of their companions. By now it was almost dark.

'We've rested sufficiently,' Jacob said. 'I think we should move.' And he swung away at the head of the flock, stepping majestically forward in the direction of the solitary rock. The sheep followed him, a dim white mass in the gloom. Jacob had calculated that, in the dark-ness, the blackened fields would not seem so menacing and he intended not to stop until these were well behind them.

They passed the rock, three or four sheep abreast. Barley, at the very back of the flock, began to mock Jacob again as she climbed. 'Just look at him – the great ram of Sweetriver – marching on without even a look round to see if we're coming. Takes us all for granted, but of course, we're only ewes.'

One of the other females looked across at her sympathetically.

Barley went on, 'He doesn't even know where he's going and here we are, meekly following him, without a murmur, as if he's a shepherd with a bale of hay!'

'Yet you raised no objection, Barley,' said the other ewe with amusement, 'when Jacob asked if we were ready.'

'What point would there have been? Mine would have been a lone voice.'

'How do you know?'

'I know ewes!'

'Well, you're one yourself, so I shouldn't be too disparaging.'

They were entering the fired area now and Barley looked at the acrid black ash that was covering her feet. She wrinkled her nose in disgust. 'On we go, on we go,' she muttered, 'through this black mess and not a word of objection from any beast.'

'Why don't you catch Jacob up and protest if you feel like that?' the other ewe inquired, rather irritably.

'Someone has to be the last sheep in the flock,' Barley answered. 'It might as well be me.'

The other ewe inwardly smiled. When it came to the crunch, there were not many of the sheep who would dare to challenge Jacob's authority.

The flock ploughed on through the wilderness and eventually Jacob could see, not far ahead, the land beginning to shelve upwards once more. Soon he and the leading sheep had reached the end of the burnt fields and, even in the darkness, they could see green growth before them. Jacob heaved a sigh of relief. His spirits lifted and he started to trot towards the rising ground, enjoying the feel of turf under his feet again. The ewes gladly increased their pace to match Jacob's. The smell of herbage and clean wet earth assailed their nostrils and they inhaled the fresh scents eagerly.

Jacob stopped and turned, waiting for the last ewe, Barley, to emerge from the blackness. 'Now we're going into new territory,' he told them. There was a definite excitement in his voice and in his whole bearing. 'No man controls the land where we're going. It's a wilder place than humans care to live in. We shall know a freedom we've never known before.'

'A freedom not to follow you, perhaps?' Barley murmured from the back.

Prancer tittered, as did another lamb, Asher, who was Reuben's friend and thought the world of him. But Reuben held his peace. He liked to think he had a maturity and dignity which set him apart from the other youngsters.

'Where can we stop to rest, Jacob?' asked Bell. 'I'm feeling tired.'

'A little further on, I think,' replied Jacob. 'We haven't come very far yet, and there are many sheep in the flock older than you.'

'I suppose Myriam would go on until she dropped if you told her to,' Bell muttered, her jealousy showing itself again.

'How do you know Jacob wasn't referring to himself?'

suggested Frolic with the cheek of a favourite child.

Jacob was delighted with this remark. 'It's true. I'm the eldest of all of you,' he laughed. 'But I'm feeling a new lease of life now: there are new prospects for us all.'

'I wonder what he means by that?' mused Barley to her neighbour. But the animal did not catch her drift.

The sheep continued on their way. In the darkness of the night some of the ewes on the outside of the flock became aware of a shadowy figure that seemed to be following them at a distance. At times it crept closer, as if reconnoitring; then it would draw away again. The mother ewes made sure their lambs were bunched in the middle of the flock where they were protected all round by the adults. 'What is it? What is it?' they whispered to each other – but the creature never came quite close enough for them to tell.

'It's a dog,' said one.

'No, no, it's too small. It's a fox,' said another.

'Dogs come in all sizes,' remarked a third.

The ghostly figure maintained its pace, sliding in and out of the shadows in a noiseless way that made the sheep more and more jittery.

'What does it want?' Barley bleated. She felt particularly vulnerable at the rear of the flock.

'Don't ask. Just keep moving,' Becky answered her.

Barley became increasingly agitated. She wished she could identify the sinister presence, but it would not approach close enough for that. It's waiting for us to stop and then it'll pounce, she kept thinking. I'm the nearest to it; it'll be me! She hurried on, trying to move further up in the flock; but the ewes in front prevented her by hurrying as well and, like a ripple passing over a pond, each line of sheep began to trot faster as it felt the one behind nudging its heels.

Jacob, out in front, was overtaken by the hurrying ewes

and lambs and he turned to see what was happening. The sheep continued to pass him, forgetting any idea of orderliness in their nervous state and completely ignoring his pleas for calm. Then he saw the cause of it all: the vague shadowy figure hovering nearby. He guessed at once it was a fox on the look-out for a sickly lamb. He decided to confront it immediately.

'You'll get no joy here, my friend,' he cried. 'There's not a weakling among us!'

The animal still kept its distance and Jacob was left behind by the flock. 'Why don't you show yourself?' he called again. 'You can't be afraid of a mere sheep.'

The animal came slowly into vision. It was indeed a fox – a young one with an immaculate coat. It seemed hesitant, faced by a powerful-looking ram; but in reality the fox was trying to keep the flock's whereabouts in view out of the corner of one eye.

'You're wasting your time pursuing us,' Jacob told him coolly.

The fox regarded him for a moment. 'That's for me to decide,' he answered. 'What are you doing so far up the valley?'

'Our pasture was flooded, of course,' said Jacob. 'Do you know nothing of the flood?'

'Certainly I know of it,' the fox replied. 'I missed the worst of it by going deep underground, though my hole was filled partly by water. And I know your flock too. You're the only sheep around here.' He was still keeping an eye on the ewes and lambs who had slowed to a walk again.

'Until you put in an appearance, I thought we were the only beasts of any sort around here,' Jacob remarked. 'The countryside is desolate. We've seen only the farm dog.'

'There was a great loss of life, I believe,' the fox

acknowledged. 'Wild creatures of all sorts were swept out of their homes or carried away by the deluge, as well as the animals your humans are interested in.'

'*My* humans?' Jacob echoed. 'You're out of date, friend. We're as free from their control as you are now.'

The fox leered. 'You might just regret telling me that,' he barked and, with a great bound, he dashed away in the wake of the tightly-packed flock.

Jacob was so surprised by his sudden disappearance that he stood and stared for a minute. Then the frantic baa-ing of the ewes as the fox ran headlong into their midst brought the ram to his senses. He galloped after.

He could see the sheep scattering, each mother trying to find its one or two young and draw them away to safety. The flock was being fragmented into a dozen little groups. This was exactly what the fox had hoped for; he wanted to isolate a lamb to give himself the best chance of a successful attack. He raced about, twisting this way and that, always aiming to separate one from the adults and cut it off.

He had miscalculated however. The lambs were big animals now of about four or five months and, frightened as they were, they had sufficient boldness to know how to help themselves without their mothers being nearby. The fox himself was frantic with the excitement of the chase and, as Jacob came up, he was running after Prancer and Dancer, the twin males. They vanished into the darkness.

Jacob looked about, wondering what he could do. Presently the fox reappeared out of the gloom, now running crazily towards him; he had evidently abandoned the twin brothers. Jacob saw the insane gleam in the fox's eyes – the animal was in an ecstasy at the havoc it was creating. But it made the mistake now of singling out Reuben to chase, veering off sharply in this lamb's direction.

Reuben stopped running abruptly and spun round to face his tormentor. He lowered his young head and the fox, unable to pull itself up, crashed straight into the budding horns. With a gasp it tumbled over twice and lay still. Reuben stared at the apparently lifeless red-brown body, and a great thrill went through him – he felt he had come of age.

But when Jacob came to look he saw the fox was not dead, it was merely badly stunned and winded. He turned to his son Reuben. Their eyes met and measured each other. Reuben was full of pride and looked almost arrogant; for the first time Jacob realized he had a rival. 'You did well, Reuben,' he forced himself to say. 'But the fox isn't dead. Now we must gather ourselves again.'

Reuben said nothing. He thought his father was attempting to mar his moment of triumph – his entry into adulthood. His admirer Asher joined him, admiration bursting from his eyes, and bleated his praise in an excited chatter. Jacob walked away.

With the fox immobilized, the flock began to congregate again. Prancer and Dancer returned and, from a safe distance, looked in amazement at the gasping creature that had put such fear into them. Asher hastened to tell them what had happened, but Reuben kept aloof.

'Reuben . . .' the twins burbled. 'Reuben . . . . But we thought Jacob—'

'Jacob only spoke to the animal,' Asher said derisively, as if giving expression to his hero's thoughts.

The twins glanced with awe at Reuben: his stocky, chubby body with its tight fleece; his erect stance; his short sturdy legs; his solid-looking head. They began to see how this lamb of their own generation could deal with such things. They felt respect for him and were aware of their own inferiority.

Jacob was busy drawing the flock together again, Jess following in his footsteps as usual. But Jess saw something in Jacob's demeanour which told him a change had come over the ram. It was a change rather beyond Jess's comprehension, yet the lamb sensed that Jacob was glad just then of his support.

Myriam saw too. When the flock was once more on the move, she went to walk with Jacob. 'The lambs are growing up,' she said.

'Some of them are no longer lambs,' Jacob replied.

From his tone Myriam could tell the subject had been on his mind before she had joined him. 'They're still lambs as far as experience goes,' she said quietly.

Jacob turned and met her eyes. He knew that she was offering him comfort. They looked at each other for a while in a warm silence. At length he said, 'Myriam, I have a feeling that there will be many more new experiences before any of us are much older.'

# —5—
# Missing

The gradient of the land lessened and soon all the animals had reached the head of the valley. They found themselves standing on level ground again and Jacob knew they had reached the wild open country of moor and heathland – now was the time for them to rest. They could begin to search out the best places to feed in the daylight. He took them to the leeside of an outcrop of limestone which rose ten metres above the ground. The sheep began to settle, needing no bidding; the events of the night had made them all weary.

As Jacob watched the less independent of the lambs nestling with their mothers, he noticed Myriam looking around uncertainly. Her puzzlement soon gave way to alarm and she ran amongst the drowsy flock, looking everywhere for Frolic. Soon she was the only ewe still on her feet.

'What is it, Myriam?' Jacob called to her.

'It's Frolic!' she cried. 'She's missing!'

'Impossible,' said Jacob, feeling his insides lurch.

'But she is, she is,' Myriam wailed in anguish.

'Jess, I thought she was walking with.'

'No. She hasn't been with me since we left the fox behind,' answered the male lamb.

'Reuben!' Jacob bleated deeply. 'Where is your sister? Did you leave her behind?'

'I thought she was with you and Myriam at the head of us all,' Reuben replied quietly – without a hint of concern in his voice.

Unmated Bridget was enjoying Myriam's anguish. She chomped away on a mouthful of herbage, presently saying unhurriedly, 'Did Frolic return after she ran away from the fox?'

Myriam froze. There was a horrible silence. Not even a breath of wind disturbed the quietness.

'No, no,' Myriam began to moan. 'Oh, no, no. I didn't see her go.'

'She ran away when the fox was chasing us all,' piped up Dancer, almost gleefully. He thought he was being helpful.

'Yes, chasing us all,' his silly brother repeated.

Now Jacob took charge. 'I'll go back, Myriam,' he said. 'I'll search for her.'

'I'll come too,' she said at once. 'I can't bear—'

'No,' Jacob interrupted. 'You stay here. It will be best for just one of us to go.'

'Please, Jacob,' she begged. 'How can I rest? Two of us could cover more ground.'

'No, Myriam,' the ram said firmly. 'You're needed here to take care of the flock. I'll find her – don't worry.' He tried to sound confident but his real feelings were quite different.

'Take care of the flock,' Barley muttered to Bridget. 'That's rich. She can't even care for one lamb.'

'Mmm.' Bridget masticated comfortably.

Jacob left at once and they saw him disappear down into the valley again. He dreaded what he might find; he knew the fox must have recovered from its blow long since and with a solitary lamb running loose . . . his lovely little Frolic . . . . Jacob shuddered. He broke into a run.

Despite the clear sky a new moon gave little light to see by and, alone, Jacob seemed to be enveloped by the darkness. He imagined how lonely and frightened Frolic must be if she was still . . . . He tried to bury the other thought and think only of how glad she would be to see her father. He called repeatedly in a breathless way as he ran awkwardly over the uneven ground.

Jacob found it difficult to understand how Myriam could have been so neglectful; she had always been such a careful mother. Of course the lambs had grown beyond the age when they needed constant care and attention, but nevertheless, he thought Myriam had been at fault for once. He shook the idea away.

'No good apportioning blame,' he murmured to himself. 'That doesn't help at all. Frolic! Fro – lic!'

Eventually Jacob was fairly sure he had arrived back at the place where the scene of general panic had occurred. He started to go more cautiously, keeping a lookout for signs of the fox as well as poor Frolic. Of course the fox was not to be seen. His breathing regulated itself and he began to call more loudly. Every moment he expected to see a white shape emerge from the shadows and run joyfully towards him – but none appeared. He thought of Myriam lying wakeful and fretful against the rocks. She would not sleep as long as he was absent; all the while she would be tormenting herself, thinking of her negligence.

The night wore on. Jacob was overcome with fatigue. He longed to lie down where he was, let his eyelids droop, and doze in the damp warm air but he knew he had to keep looking and calling. Frolic was not particularly intelligent and he wondered what she would have decided to do once she was safe from the fox. For one awful moment it occurred to Jacob that Frolic might have tried to return to her home pasture – but he soon discounted it. She would be too afraid of encountering Kep.

Dawn began to break, but the early birdsong was the only evidence of life anywhere around. Jacob had wandered all night and was ready to drop. He lay down by some tussocks of bent grass and drowsed, waiting for daylight.

When he opened his eyes again it was as if to a horrible dream. The first thing he saw was the fox standing only a little way off, watching him curiously. The animal had eaten – there was the unmistakable stain of blood on its muzzle and the strong odour of male fox tainted the air. Jacob jumped up at once.

'I thought it was you,' the fox said slowly. 'But you looked different lying down, with your eyes shut.'

'What do you want?' Jacob demanded, not knowing how to answer.

'Nothing . . . now,' the fox replied with emphasis. Jacob's blood ran cold.

'I'm for shelter and some sleep now the sun's up,' the hunter went on. 'I was on the way home when I spotted you.'

Jacob forced himself to ask what he dreaded to hear. 'You haven't seen—' he began, but his voice shook.

'A young sheep? Oh yes,' the fox drawled. Jacob's heart sank. 'She's got herself in a proper pickle, hasn't she?'

'What . . . what . . . do you mean?' stammered the ram.

'Don't you know?'

'Of course not!' Jacob's exasperation and anxiety boiled over. 'I've been combing the valley all night without success! Where is this sheep? Are you sure it's the one I'm looking for?'

'I dunno. I haven't seen any other sheep about – not since last night, anyway,' the fox added as an afterthought.

'Where is she then?' asked Jacob, as humbly as he could.

'She's fallen down a little gully – in the dark, I suppose,' the fox said unfeelingly. 'Must have missed her footing. You won't be able to do anything for her, I couldn't get at her myself – er, to see if I could help I mean,' he added hastily.

Jacob was not fooled. 'Pah! A strange world where foxes try to rescue sheep,' he said bitterly. 'Where is this gully – will you show me?'

'Softened your tone a bit now, haven't you?' the fox said, leering at Jacob. 'All right. I'll point you in the direction anyway. Though why I should after what happened last night . . . .'

'You smell of gore,' Jacob told him with distaste.

'So what? I have to eat, don't I? A nice plump rabbit for a change; they're hard to find these days.'

'I'm not interested in your hunting stories, fox,' said Jacob. 'Just show me the way and we'll dispense with each other's company.'

'All right. Follow me, ram,' the fox said sarcastically.

He moved off with a loose sort of lope and Jacob urged his tired legs to run after him. The sun was shining again and Jacob welcomed its warmth on his stiffened muscles and sinews. It was the third day since the flood. The fox ran for about half a kilometre; then he stopped. The ram followed with laboured breath, his barrel of a body heaving desperately – the fox eyed him with amusement.

'Getting a bit old for these sorts of games, aren't you?' he asked drily.

Jacob gasped. 'Yes, my . . . wind's not . . . what it was.'

'Well, after you've recovered,' the fox said cheekily, 'you go on to that lone hawthorn tree. Under its roots the ground sort of splits in two. There's a crack in the rock; that's where she is.'

'Is . . . is she injured?' Jacob panted.

'Couldn't tell you. Not my concern,' the fox answered abruptly. He yawned and scratched his belly with a hind leg, 'I'm away now,' and ran off without a backward glance.

Jacob walked disconsolately towards the tree, dreading what he might find. The branches were laden with green haws. There was a narrow chasm underneath the tree's gnarled, half-exposed roots, and Frolic was wedged about halfway down on a sort of rocky ledge. She was facing away from Jacob and her body seemed to be quite motionless. She did not stir as he approached. 'Frolic,' he called, gently.

A ripple of awareness ran along the flesh of her back, but she made no sound.

'Are you hurt?'

A faint answer came, 'Jacob?'

'Yes. Can you move?'

'I . . . can't move,' Frolic bleated, her voice full of fear. 'I might fall further—'

'Can you turn? Are your legs—'

'No!' she cried, her terror freezing her into immobility. 'I daren't, Jacob.'

Jacob paused. Then he said, very softly and calmly, 'Are your legs broken?'

'No, I jarred them when I fell, that's all. But don't make me move, Jacob!'

'All right, all right, Frolic,' he soothed. 'I only want to help you.'

'You can't help me!' the poor creature cried. 'I can't get out and no other animal can get in.'

Here was an awful problem indeed and Jacob had no answer for it. He thought of Myriam waiting through the night for him to return. He felt he must get back to the flock, yet how could he walk away? He tried to think clearly but Frolic was his favourite lamb and it was difficult not to let his anxiety get the better of him. At last he had to recognize his helplessness: he could achieve nothing even if he should stay by his daughter for the rest of the day.

'Listen, Frolic,' he said slowly, trying to keep his voice even. 'I must get back to Myriam and tell her what has happened. I left the flock in her charge. But I will return – I hope before nightfall – when I've decided what to do.' He hated the emptiness of his words.

Frolic gave no answer. She knew her father was beaten; there was nothing to say.

The sun was well up when the exhausted ram once more reached the rocks where he had left the other sheep. Myriam had been watching his approach for a long time. She alone had not moved from the resting place, the other ewes and the lambs were grazing quite a way off amongst a number of wild ponies. Only Jess was nearby.

Myriam was prepared for the worst since Jacob was unaccompanied and she allowed him to regain his breath and composure. He lay down against one of the great boulders and told her what he had seen.

'All is lost then,' said Myriam. 'She'll die of starvation.'

'I haven't given up yet,' Jacob said. 'There's still a chance. But I can do no more – for the present.' His head was bowing even as he spoke.

'You must rest,' Myriam said with compassion. 'I'll let you be.'

'You must rest too,' Jacob said drowsily. 'Have you slept at all?'

'Scarcely,' she admitted. 'But I will now. The flock will be safe among the ponies – and I told them only to graze where they were.'

'Very wise,' Jacob mumbled. And he was asleep.

Myriam dozed by his side until dark. Some of the flock were mingling around her as she stood up – her movement woke Jacob.

'Dusk already,' he muttered and immediately remembered his last words to Frolic. 'I must go.'

Myriam looked at him questioningly.

'I'm going back to Frolic,' he explained. 'I promised.'

'But Jacob, what can you do?' Myriam whispered.

'I can do nothing myself,' he admitted. 'But I have an idea that another creature can.'

'Who? What can you mean?'

'I mean Kep,' he answered calmly. 'By now she might have found the master and a good sheepdog will always tell the shepherd when a sheep is in danger.'

'But Kep knows nothing of Frolic's danger.'

'That's why I have to go.'

'All the way back to the farm?'

'If I have to, Myriam. We haven't travelled so very far.'

'Let me go with you this time,' she beseeched him. 'I could stay with Frolic.'

Jacob looked at her pensively. 'I wish you could. But the flock would wander with neither of us here.'

Jess had been listening avidly to the adults. He longed to play some part in this adventure but his timidity had held him back. At last he broke in, 'Jacob, I can go with you. I'll go all the way – I'm not tired.'

Jacob began to refuse him. 'No, no, Jess—'

But Myriam interrupted him, 'Why not? He'll come to no harm with you, and it's a long, lonely trek back.'

'You're not his mother ewe, Myriam.'

'No, but Bell cares no more for him than a blade of grass – she's more interested in trying to catch your eye.' Luckily Bell was out of earshot.

'Very well, Jess,' said Jacob. 'But I want no trouble.

You're to be on your best behaviour, I have enough on my mind without—'

'Yes, yes,' cried the excited male lamb. 'Whatever you say, Jacob. I'll be like a little mole; you won't even know I'm around.'

'Come then.'

Jacob drew some cud from his stomach to chew as he walked. Jess followed behind, so close he could almost step on the ram's hocks. The lamb felt elated; only he out of all the flock was permitted to go with his father. He thought of himself as being selected for a special task – only half grown up, his young head was full of dreams.

Jacob did not speak a word until, in the gloaming, he had managed to find the lone hawthorn tree. 'Tread carefully her, Jess. It's dangerous,' he said. 'Stay this side of the branches. I'll go and talk to Frolic.'

The wretched ewe lamb was still on the ledge, but Jacob could see that she had found room to kneel down, sheep-fashion, to rest her legs. She appeared to be waiting with resignation for her end.

'Frolic!' called Jacob. 'I've returned and I have a plan.' Frolic's ears twitched but she made no reply.

'I'm going to get help for you,' her father resumed.

'Jacob,' she replied, her voice flat and hopeless. 'my death is inevitable. Only Man could save me from it.'

'That is my plan,' Jacob told her.

For a moment Frolic's despair seemed to lift a little, 'But how . . . how could it be done?'

Jacob did not want to mention the role of the collie in his plan. 'Trust me,' he said simply. 'I've come to keep you company through the dark hours. Jess is with me too. At dawn I shall go to seek the aid of Man.'

Frolic's head drooped. She thought there was scant chance of success.

Jacob lay down and prepared for sleep, not yet recovered from his wanderings on the previous night. Jess came to join him, nibbling at the turf around him, and saw that the ram was very tired. He himself felt wakeful; he waited for Jacob to fall asleep. It was not a long wait.

Jess looked at his father; even in sleep he was a noble-looking animal. The lamb would do anything to earn the ram's respect and admiration, and he thought he knew of a way in which he could do that. Poor Jacob was worn out and he faced another long trek at dawn to find Kep. What if he could be saved the effort? Would not he be pleased and grateful?

'I could go,' Jess said to himself. 'I know the way home. I'm not tired a bit; I could bring the dog back here before dawn. What a surprise for Jacob!'

Jess could not restrain himself from having a little skip round in his delight at his own cleverness. Then he made sure his father was still sleeping. Saying nothing to Frolic he set his head in the homeward direction. The night had grown very dark.

Full of confidence and excitement át his boldness, Jess cantered down the valley – no thought of foxes or any other dangers in his head. He could think only of the moment of jubilation when he would present himself with Kep at first light to the amazed Jacob. Jess was exultant at the prospect; it was to be his moment. How he was to find the bitch and persuade her to follow him for his own purposes he had not even considered.

# —6—

# A Leap at Dawn

Kep had not eaten for four days. In vain she had waited for her master to come back for her, gnawed by loneliness, frustrated by the barrier of water, miserable, sad and ravenously hungry. Her appearance was pitiful: she looked unkempt, thin and rather wild. She knew nothing about her master's and mistress's stay in hospital and their utter homelessness, she only knew that her master was alive and she could not understand why he had abandoned her.

She had turned hunter in the absence of her usual source of food but, although she hunted, she found nothing but water and vegetation. Kep had little idea of hunting methods and even less of what she should hunt for. In the early hours of the fourth day after the flood she was still fasting.

In the darkness she ranged beyond the home fields. She knew her master would not come looking for her in the dark, but as soon as the first faint glimmer of light showed in the morning the collie would return as close to home as she could, to wait patiently through the day for some sign of him. So whilst Jess was crossing the burnt fields on his way to search for her, Kep was running half-heartedly up the valley in search of food.

It was still a little time before dawn when their paths crossed. Kep spotted the lamb first and immediately sank to her belly and froze. Although she remembered her training, after four days without food all other thoughts and feelings were swallowed up by the one great dominating urge to eat. Watching the plump male lamb, Kep's mouth ran with water. Presently Jess saw her.

He was not entirely sure at first if it was Kep watching him. She looked different but her attitude was familiar.

'Kep?' he bleated uncertainly.

Kep gulped hard. Her hunger-racked body ached with a painful emptiness. In a hard shrill tone she yapped, 'Yes.'

The lamb approached closer. Kep tensed; she was preparing to pounce. Jess could not see the strange glare in the bitch's eyes.

'I've come . . . we need . . . I need your help,' he said finally. He was not certain how to proceed.

Kep let her muscles relax. Were her ears playing tricks on her?

'Say it again!' she barked, and swallowed several times.

'I want you to go with me,' said Jess innocently.

Kep gave a growling laugh. 'Oh yes,' she muttered. 'I'll go with you – just you try and stop me.'

Jess was puzzled. There was something strange about Kep's manner. 'You . . . you seem d-different,' he stammered, beginning to feel frightened.

Kep's eyes narrowed and she swished her tail. She was calculating the distance between them.

'You see, Frolic is trapped and . . . and . . . we . . . Jacob, that is, wanted you to get the m-master,' Jess blurted out.

Kep was caught off her guard. For a moment the image of her master re-entered her consciousness. 'What's this all about?' she growled.

Jess explained hastily.

Kep understood – but her hunger asserted itself again and blocked out any other consideration. A new prospect opened up before her of two unguarded lambs. She could spring at Jess now, it would all be over in a trice; she had the strength of desperation in her. But then she would not know where the other lamb was and, in her present precarious existence, two good meals were better than one. If she could just be patient a little longer, the reward at the end would be worth waiting for. 'You'd better show me then,' she said softly. She was a clever dog and made no mention of the fact that she had not found her master.

Poor Jess was too young and naive to think of asking her. Now his initial trepidation was over, he could only think once more of his triumphant return to Jacob and Frolic. With a frisky little jump he turned himself round to head back to the burnt fields. Without another sound Kep trailed him, watching the lamb's plump hindquarters and salivating copiously. The cunning collie meant to follow Jess only as far as she needed to discover the whereabouts of the other young sheep – then, silently and suddenly, she would pull him down.

During the night Frolic bleated, seeking the reassurance of Jacob's answer – but Jacob still slept. Then Frolic called out to Jess. When he also failed to reply she decided they must both be asleep. So she slept also. Then towards dawn, she awoke with a start, feeling ill at ease; she could sense all was not well. She knew nothing of the approach of the ravenous sheepdog, yet she scented danger in the air: she bleated loudly.

At last Jacob awoke, 'What is it, Frolic?' he mumbled drowsily.

'I don't know,' she answered, her voice tense.

Jacob raised himself and immediately noticed Jess's

absence. He called him irritably.

'I think he's wandered off,' said Frolic. 'He hasn't spoken a single word to me since you arrived.'

'Oh, I knew it was a mistake bringing him!' Jacob cried angrily. 'I shouldn't have relented. In future I shall trust only my own judgement. The ewes—'

Frolic interrupted him. 'It's growing light,' she said. 'Maybe you'll find him when you go for help.'

'Yes, and maybe not,' her father muttered. 'And if not, he must look out for himself. I'll search for no more lambs!'

There was sufficient light for him to see Frolic now. He stood for a moment longer, before setting off. Suddenly, in the greyness of early dawn, he saw something in the chasm he had not detected before. There was an indentation in the rock on the opposite side to where Frolic had slipped, higher up than the ledge on which she was lying. As Jacob looked at it he could see that there would be just room enough for an animal the size of Frolic to stand in it. Above this indentation, a scrubby patch of ling and bramble hung down covering a patch of rock where the plants' roots were embedded in a fissure. In an instant the ram realized that if Frolic were to use all her natural nimble-footedness and balancing skill she could climb out of the gulley. But first she would have to jump from the ledge to the indentation in the opposite side of the chasm. It would certainly be a risk, for if she should slip she would go crashing to the bottom. Jacob, however, thought it was a risk worth taking.

'Frolic,' he said softly but with a noticeable excitement, 'I think I can see your escape route.'

'Oh. Is he coming?' Thinking that the sheep farmer approached she got hastily to her feet.

'No,' said Jacob. 'Better than that. You can do it yourself!'

'Oh, Jacob,' she answered. 'I can't. How cruel of you to raise my hopes.' In Frolic's voice there was bitter disappointment.

'Frolic, my cherished daughter,' Jacob said tenderly, 'I would never tease you in that way. Believe me, there is a way out for you; I've only just discovered it. Look across at the rock on the other side – do you see?'

'No,' said Frolic sullenly.

'Surely you can see that the rock there isn't sheer like this end where you slipped?'

'I can see a sort of hole – but what use is that to me?'

'You could jump across the chasm and then scramble into that undergrowth, you'd soon be able to haul yourself—'

'No! No!' she cried in horror. 'I couldn't. I could never do that!'

'You could,' urged Jacob.

But Frolic would not budge. She had the memory of one sudden fall; it was enough to deter her from chancing another. Instead she asked Jacob to do what he had promised to do – to fetch human help. She trusted in that: Man could do anything.

Jacob saw that persuasion was useless. He sighed and, as the light broadened, he cropped some mouthfuls of turf. Then he moved slowly away. In the distance he could see two animals approaching.

Kep's powerful sense of smell told her of Jacob's proximity before she could see him. There was no mistaking the scent of the ram. Now she guessed she must be very close to where the she-lamb was trapped. The bitch knew she must soon make her attack. She wanted no hindrance from Jacob; she held his strength and tenacity in too much respect to dare a kill within his range.

When Jess spied the heavy stocky figure of his father he started to run. Kep knew it was now or never. With bared fangs she sprang from behind and the weight of her bowled the lamb over. But the dog had underestimated the lamb's strength; with a bleat of terror Jess kicked out viciously with his hind feet and caught the dog a blow on one shoulder. Kep reeled a little and Jess struggled to his feet and raced away. Jacob was now close enough to see the attack and he came thundering down towards them. Kep snarled in frustration and tore after the lamb to pull him down before the ram could intervene, but Jess had made straight for his father's protection and Kep realized that, even should she catch him, she would have Jacob to deal with before she could drag her prey away to a safe spot.

She halted, panting uncertainly. Then she had an idea and laughed to herself. She could still outwit them and not lose her feast. Jess might have escaped, but there was one lamb who could not do so! The lamb in the trap was her quarry – all she had to do was find the bait.

Kep ran easily round the two sheep keeping a good few metres distance, then loped on towards where she reckoned Frolic must be. Together Jess and Jacob watched her. While Jess explained to his father why he had disappeared, Kep neared the lone hawthorn and the gulley. The dog paused to sniff the late summer morning. The smell of sheep was everywhere, but she picked up Jacob's old scent and followed it along the ground. With a bark of triumph she saw the chasm.

Frolic shivered at the sound. Like all the sheep she was wary of Kep, but she thought the dog had come accompanied. She heard a scraping sound as Kep's front feet scratched the rock; she was nosing into the chasm, searching for a safe way in. Then the collie withdrew hastily, growling with annoyance. She saw the ledge, she saw the lamb and – with exasperation – she saw the long drop to the bottom. She knew any attempt to get at the sheep would be futile. Hunger and despair drove her frantic and, in a fury, she raced around the chasm barking wildly.

Now Frolic knew something was amiss. She heard no voices, nor Jacob's deep comforting bleats. The dog had come not to save her but to kill her! She heard Kep's feet scrabbling again at the rock, beside herself with rage. Frolic quivered and quaked, waiting for the searing fangs to strike at her. Then suddenly, without thinking, the terror-struck lamb leaped out into space, her legs gathered under her and, with a thump, landed on the indented piece of rock her father had discovered. For an instant she teetered on the brink, feet flailing for a hold. Then she was safe, wedged into the hole, and staring across at Kep who peered at her from the rim.

'You'll never escape,' the dog growled. 'I shall be waiting here to pounce.'

Frolic was too frightened to reply. She stood silently, quivering with fear.

Then the bleats of Jess and Jacob reached them, and Kep dropped to her belly. She knew she was beaten. Jess held back when he saw the dog lying by the lip of the chasm, but he was quite safe. There was no fight left in Kep, and Jacob advanced slowly.

'All right, Kep,' he said quietly. 'You've tried to turn sheep killer and you've failed. Why don't you just go?'

Kep got up; she had no choice. 'Yes, I'll go,' she said. 'But I'll be back some time – you'll never know when. You have to sleep, but you won't rest soundly, I promise you! One night, somewhere, I'll steal up . . . .'

Jacob bent his brows and made a move towards her; Kep was not foolish enough to stay any longer. As she loped off, she snarled at him, 'Remember my words!'

Jess rejoined his father, who had not reprimanded him for his disobedience. The lamb had meant well and had certainly learnt his lesson. Together they went to speak to Frolic, and Jacob was amazed to see her halfway to freedom.

'Frolic, my brave ewe lamb!' he bleated loudly.

'It was the dog – I jumped from fright,' she explained.

'Now then, one more jump,' Jacob pleaded. 'A jump for liberty!'

Jess added his voice. 'Only a little one, Frolic, and we're all united again.'

Frolic inched herself round and weighed up the situation. She saw the purple heather and thick growth of bramble which she must reach. The distance was not so great as that she had jumped already and it was this that decided her. Gathering herself together, she launched herself outwards, scrambling for a foothold on the vegetation and then pulling – straining upwards until she stood once more on firm land.

She was hungry and very thirsty, and at once Jacob hurried her and Jess back to find the rest of the flock.

Myriam was overjoyed to see the three of them. She could hardly believe the story of Frolic's adventure and of her narrow escape from the collie. But when Jess took Frolic to the nearest drinking place, his mother, Bell, merely glanced across from where she was feeding.

'So you're back,' she said, without interest.

Jess did not answer – he had no feeling for her any longer. His recent experiences had removed the last of his filial affection, and only his father retained a claim on him. He felt himself to be a mature lamb.

Jacob looked around him to see if the flock had stayed together.

'I've managed to prevent most of them from straying,' Myriam told him. 'Only a few have wandered.'

'You did well, Myriam,' Jacob commented. 'Are the lambs safe?'

'They've all stayed close by, and their mother ewes too.'

'Have you found good feeding?'

'It's patchy, Jacob. Now we're reunited, you could lead us on.'

'I intend to,' he said. 'Let's get everyone together.'

He and Myriam bleated to the flock which mingled around them gladly.

'Those sheep who have chosen to go their own way must fend for themselves from now on,' Jacob announced decisively. 'We'll waste no more time. Most of you are here, and it's safer for all of us to stay around each other. We can warn one another of danger and, in a mass, we're less likely to be attacked.' He thought for a moment of Kep's parting warning, but he kept it to himself. 'We're entering a wilder sort of country,' he went on, 'with no protection from Man any more. But we'll manage, never fear. Together we'll manage.'

Jacob's steadfast, fearless expression reassured the flock, inspiring them with confidence. Then he turned and marched off at their head. The ram was an impressive figure: even Barley was hushed.

By noon, though the sheep were unaware of it, they had entered within the bounds of Leckmoor National Park.

# —7—
# A Warning

Kep had one more day and night of misery to endure. She returned to her home area, flitting to and fro. The waters had receded and, in the village, reclamation operations were well under way. But Kep's passage was still barred by a great lake of floodwater she was too weak to swim. That night, as she lay disconsolately within sight of her master's ruined home, a weasel ran past her very nose. She snapped at it mechanically and broke its neck, but it provided only a poor meal and seemed to aggravate her hunger. She no longer expected to see her master but, with the daylight, she still waited on, head on paws.

She was drowsing in the sunlight when, as if in a dream, she saw him clambering out of a dinghy at the edge of the newly formed lake and wading towards her. She got up hesitantly.

Talbot was hesitant too – was this Kep? He called her name and the dog bounded forward, splashing through the puddles. Talbot began to sob as he bent down to hug her, feeling her ribs. Then he swung her up and carried her to the rubber boat where another man sat waiting. His friend, a cattle farmer from a neighbouring area which had escaped the worst of the flood, paddled them away. Talbot looked around at the wreckage and the strangeness, and his sobs became louder. Not another creature could be seen. But Kep had lost her wildness: she was a sheepdog again.

Amongst the heather, the gorse and the bracken the Sweetriver flock wandered on, seeking out the purple moor grasses to graze. The ground was still spongy and wet in most places and there were bogs too, where peat moss proliferated. But Jacob indicated what was safest to eat and the sheep saw sense.

For a while Jacob was a hero. His selflessness in searching for his daughter and restoring her to the flock was judged remarkable by the ewes. And Jess, as his companion, basked in the reflected glory. When Frolic heard the history of her half-brother's brave journey alone in the night to fetch help, she saw him through new eyes: the two lambs became inseparable.

But it was Barley, as usual, who struck the first discordant note among the roaming flock. She was becoming tired of the other ewes' dumb obedience and started to question the ram's loyalty. 'It seems to have been forgotten that, having found his precious Frolic, he left other sheep behind,' she remarked. 'Puts himself out for his favourites, doesn't he, but otherwise—'

'He couldn't search out every individual sheep in this vast area, could he?' one of the ewes reasoned. 'They shouldn't have strayed so far.'

'He spent long enough on one stray,' Barley bleated.

Frolic overheard. 'I didn't stray,' she defended herself. 'I had an accident.'

'Yes, yes, we're all familiar with your story,' Barley sneered. 'Maybe some of those other sheep have had accidents by now as well!'

Bridget had been chewing thoughtfully. 'I can see Barley's point,' she said in her slow way. 'The ram has his faults.'

'One of them being that he didn't choose to mate with you, I suppose,' Bell suggested acidly.

Bridget chewed on, but the words had stung.

'O great infallible Jacob,' chanted Barley, 'may we be permitted to have some control over our lives?'

Myriam turned her head, amused despite herself, but Jacob marched on, regardless. Dancer and Prancer sniggered.

'Jacob's harem,' Barley muttered as the flock went on.

The sun continued to beam down, drying out the countryside. In the wide open stretches of moor, heath and marsh, the flock began to split up. The weather was kind, there were no visible bounds to their feeding area, and Jacob's words were forgotten in the absence of any obvious danger. With each day, the numbers of the main flock dwindled.

Of the lambs, it was Reuben who was the first to bridle under Jacob's authority. 'I'm fed up with being herded about,' he told Asher, his admirer. 'Jacob forgets his age. I may have to challenge him when the time is right, he can't lord it over the rest of the males for ever.'

Asher's heart beat faster as he heard these daring words. The prospect of dissension made his skin crawl with excitement – to see Jacob ousted!

'We're no longer lambs,' Reuben added.

'No indeed,' Asher agreed. But he was not as fast a developer as his big companion and he did not really understand Reuben's talk. Asher still felt and thought like a lamb – to hear himself described as a young male was a thrilling notion with which he was not yet able to identify.

On occasion the flock would see other domesticated creatures – usually lone animals who had somehow survived the flood and who wandered aimlessly in the absence of human control. They saw a horse, with a donkey as his companion; another time a tabby cat and also a small pig.

This pig had a covering of short reddish hair. Its body was lean and it trotted towards the flock in a springy, inquisitive sort of way. 'First sheep I've seen,' it told them. 'Did you run from the flood like me?'

'Not run,' Jacob said. 'We were saved by our position – but we had to move up here to find food.'

'I had to swim,' the pig went on. 'The piggery was flooded out. They all drowned; I'm the only survivor.' He sounded quite proud of the fact.

'Lucky indeed,' Myriam remarked.

'I've no owners,' said the pig. 'They all went away. I'm not used to being solitary – don't like it much. And there's very little to eat here.'

'What do you feed on?' asked Jacob, politely.

'Roots, bulbs, grubs, insects . . . but I can't seem to get a really good meal inside me.'

'I don't think we can help you,' Jacob said doubtfully.

'Wasn't asking for help,' the pig retorted. 'But you don't object to company?'

'Of course not,' said Jacob, still feeling doubtful.

'My name's Carl,' said the pig. 'I'm a curiosity, you know – an old breed.'

He trotted about, examining the fleeces of several of the flock, his mischievous little eyes darting from one animal to another. 'Warm work for you in the sun,' he observed.

'We were shorn some weeks ago,' Jacob said. 'It's not too bad for us.'

'Were you? Your fleeces do grow quickly. My word! Not much wool covering me – ha ha!' Carl grunted, enjoying his joke.

The sheep exchanged glances amongst themselves.

They were not quite sure what to make of the pig.

'He's like a bald creature,' muttered Reuben, who had never seen a pig.

'He's very ugly,' murmured Bell.

Carl did not hear. 'Wonderful how you all keep together, you sheep,' he observed. 'It must be very reassuring to be in a large group.'

'It is,' said Jacob. 'That's why I try to see we remain as a flock.'

'Oh, I see. You're the leader, are you?' Carl said.

'Self-appointed,' bleated Barley.

Carl was amused. 'Is there some unrest here?' he chortled.

Jacob was irritated. He was used to Barley's gibes, but he objected to the pig being a witness to one.

'Nothing of any importance,' he said in his deep clear voice.

Prancer made his face very grave. He turned to his brother, 'No importance,' he intoned. Dancer giggled delightedly, and they skipped about, trying to copy the quick little steps of the pig.

The brothers were quietened by Reuben. 'Grow up!' he demanded fiercely, and their awe of him made them obey him.

Carl said to the flock in general, 'Are you heading in any particular direction?'

The ewes automatically waited for Jacob to reply. But the ram merely looked pensive, saying nothing.

'Well, Jacob?' prompted Barley. 'Where are we heading? Only you can tell us!'

Jacob drew himself up and looked at the cluster of white woolly bodies. 'It's not so much a question of where we're heading,' he told them, 'as of maintaining our well-being. We're a healthy flock of animals and we've been pretty lucky. We want to keep it that way – find the best food, the best shelter and keep clear of our enemies. For conditions won't always be as kind as this.'

'What do you expect then?' Bell asked.

'Things to be more of a challenge to us,' Jacob replied mysteriously. He turned to the pig. 'You have very little in common with us,' he remarked. 'But if you really are seeking company, I don't think any of us would have any objection to your remaining nearby.'

Carl snorted with satisfaction. 'Thank you, Jacob,' he said. 'Who knows, I might be of some use to you.'

'I doubt it,' Reuben muttered.

Carl thought it was time to make himself scarce. 'I may see you tomorrow,' he said and trotted off with a light step, full of curiosity at everything around him.

'I don't like pigs,' remarked Bridget. 'Never did. Little sly eyes – you never know what they're thinking.'

'I think he's quite harmless,' said Becky.

'Well, I don't trust him,' the fat ewe declared.

Over the next few days they saw quite a lot of Carl; but he always kept his distance. They saw him rooting amongst the heather or lying in the bracken, snoozing. Once they saw him wallowing in a marsh, emitting a series of the most ecstatic grunts. The pig always kept near the sheep as if comforted by their proximity, and for the most part, they ignored him.

The weather changed very suddenly towards the end of August. The air became much colder and a mist developed, blown in from the sea. Sometimes the sheep became separated in the poor visibility and the flock became further depleted: it now numbered around forty sheep.

The difficult weather conditions seemed to encourage predators, who seemed to have been waiting for a change. From time to time, through a break in the mist, they saw the dim shape of a buzzard wheeling nearby. The hawks shadowed them more in hope than with any definite design, waiting to see if an animal would fall sick or make a mistake. A healthy, full-grown sheep was usually safe enough, but in the mist, in boggy country, a slip might occur. Foxes, too, were on the prowl. The ewes became nervous for the lambs but, even with extra vigilance, one of them wandered too far off and lost sight of the main group. They heard it bleating in the night hours but it was too risky to search in the darkness. In the morning Carl found the flock and told them two foxes had made a kill. 'One of yours, no question,' he grunted.

'Inevitable,' Jacob remarked. 'It was only a matter of time; we've been unusually lucky till now.'

As the mother of the missing lamb had not been seen for many days there was no further comment on the incident. But for a time the flock was more tightly knit. At night they huddled together and Jacob or Myriam kept watch – they frequently saw foxes skulking close.

The mists gave way to rain – not rain like that that had fallen and caused the flood, but steady, unremitting drizzle that gave the landscape a dull, cheerless look. But the flock's fleeces shed water easily and they were not bothered by it; they munched resolutely on.

One day one of the hardy moorland ponies spoke to Jacob. 'You're in for a tough time if you plan to stay on the moors.'

'I wouldn't dispute that,' replied Jacob.

'Yes,' said the pony, a brown stocky stallion with short, sturdy legs and a barrel chest, 'winter here is an ordeal that few animals of your sort could imagine.'

'Winter's a long way off,' said Jacob.

'It comes early some years,' remarked the pony. 'I'm

just warning you, since you're not a native of the moors. Feeding becomes a constant problem then. You'd do well to consider that.'

'Are you thinking we might be competition perhaps?' Jacob asked subtly.

'Yes and no,' the pony answered. 'I'm surprised men haven't come to round you up. Since they haven't, they may not know you're here – before winter you might wish that they did.'

Jacob considered. 'We'll see,' he murmured.

'Some years the snow is so thick that animals are buried alive,' the pony went on. 'I remember one such time – only we ponies survived it. Foxes and small animals starved to death, a lot of ponies did too. I don't know how sheep could cope?'

'Neither do I,' Jacob admitted. 'Thank you for your warning, even if it is a little premature.'

'All right then,' the pony said, wandering off.

Jacob was certain the animal was acting in the interests of its own kind, hoping to conserve its grazing grounds – but that was absurd in such a vast area! He told Myriam about it.

'I'm sure you're right,' she agreed. 'In the winter any grass is bound to be in short supply. But I wonder if the men will come to look for us?'

'We don't know what happened to them. Kep couldn't find the master, and now the flock is scattered. We're all marked beasts, but when our fleeces really grow the marks will be hard to spot. I think we're quite safe from intervention.'

'Sometimes,' said Myriam, 'I wonder if we should have strayed so far.'

'We had to find pasture,' Jacob insisted. 'And aren't you pleased not to lose your lambs? They would have been taken long ago . . . .'

'Yes – I know it. But we're not wild creatures, and if that pony is right about winters, we might live to regret this independence.'

'Oh, you ewes,' Jacob chided her. 'Worry, worry, worry. Winter doesn't come in a day; don't fret about things that might never happen.'

They heard no more from the pony, and the flock roamed the moorland at will until they reached the fringe of the forest.

'There would be a place to shelter from winter weather,' Myriam observed, as they looked at the dark mass of pine trees that seemed impenetrable.

'It had occurred to me too,' Jacob said. 'But there would be nothing to eat there. Do you see how bare the ground is underneath?'

'I do.'

'But we must remember it. It could serve us well for a short time. Better to go without food for a while than to be buried alive!'

# —8—
# A Helping Hand

Autumn came early on Leckmoor. Rowan and thorn shed their bright yellow leaves, and gales roared over the moors, tossing the spiky gorse and tearing at the heather and grass. These were cold grim days, giving a foretaste of what was to come.

Then September passed, and for a week or two in October there was a sort of Indian Summer – the sun shone again and the days were calm. Carl made a reappearance, having spent most of his time previously sheltering from the gales. 'This is better; better by far,' he commented one very warm day. He lay on his side amongst the recumbent sheep in the sunniest spot he could find. He had lost a lot of weight.

'Make the most of it,' said Jacob. He had passed on to the pig the pony's forewarning about winter.

'I mean to,' said Carl.

'What will you do afterwards?'

Carl stretched and lifted a leg in an attempt to locate a spot he wanted to scratch. Then he said, 'Fatten myself up first. I'll go to the forest you mentioned – bound to be nuts and mushrooms and such like in there. Then I'll be better equipped for the hard months.'

'I hope you're not underestimating those hard months,' Jacob said with misgiving. 'You haven't got a lot covering you.'

'No, only my thick skin!' grunted Carl good-naturedly. He got up. 'I'm too hot now – I need to cool off. I must find a place to wallow.' He trotted off.

Dancer and Prancer, who were bored, decided to follow the pig. To them he was a figure of fun, and they had the idea that Carl's wallowing would be a source of much amusement. They kept a distance behind him, bleating their usual nonsense to each other.

Carl was looking out for a growth of rushes. He knew that where these plants grew the ground was likely to be marshy, and this was just what he required. Presently, the young brother sheep saw him stop and snout around on the ground for a while. Then the pig took a few steps forward and suddenly he was up to his belly in mud! Snorting with delight Carl crashed around, rolling on to his side and really covering himself with as much of the mud as he could. Dancer and Prancer looked at each other in astonishment. It seemed to them that the pig had completely lost his wits. But Carl's little blue-grey eyes saw them watching him.

'It's wonderful!' he called. 'A real tonic!'

He floundered around a little longer and then heaved his glistening body out on to firm ground. He gave himself a liberal shaking and lumps of mud flew in all directions.

'I suppose you two think I look comical?' he asked the sheep amiably.

'Out of your mind,' Dancer replied rudely. 'Why do you do it?'

Carl grunted. 'You'd have to be a pig to understand,' he answered. 'And since you're not . . . .' He trotted off, feeling cool and comfortable, pleased with his bath.

Prancer looked at Dancer. 'Shall we investigate?' he prompted.

'Can if you like. Don't think there's much to see.'

'Come on, Dancer.'

'All right.'

The sheep went forward cautiously and found that the rushes parted as they stepped through. 'Phew!' said Dancer. 'There's a strong smell.'

'That's what attracts the pig,' cried Prancer, and the two silly animals collapsed again into giggles. Their merriment was infectious – the more one giggled, the more the other followed suit, louder and louder, until they no longer paid any attention to their footing. It happened in a moment: Prancer, who led the way, found himself sinking into the soggy marshland. He panicked and tried to find a way out, but only felt himself sinking deeper.

'Help, Dancer, help!' he cried in terror. 'It's trying to swallow me! Get the pig, get the pig!'

Dancer had the worst sort of character for an emergency appeal of this kind. Neither he nor his brother had any good sense or maturity and, seeing the danger his brother was in, Dancer simply turned tail and fled before he too should be engulfed.

Prancer's bleats became more frantic as his struggles became weaker. More and more of his body sank into the mud and the smell of the stagnant bog and its rotting vegetation nearly stifled him.

When Dancer raced towards the flock alone, it was immediately obvious to the other sheep something had gone wrong; the two brother sheep were never seen out of each other's company. The frightened Dancer could not be calmed down – he ran round in circles, ignoring the calls of the adults, including his mother Becky.

Carl, who was allowing his mud coat to dry on him in the sun, had an inkling of what might have happened. He knew perfectly well that one had to choose just the right place in a boggy area for safety. He lay still for a moment, wondering if he really was sufficiently interested in the welfare of two silly sheep to bother himself. He had just decided that he was not, and was composing himself to slumber when, all at once, he remembered what he had said to Jacob at their first meeting. 'I might be of some use to you . . . .'

'I suppose I'd better go and see,' he muttered. 'Though I don't expect I'll be able to do anything.'

Dancer had stopped running. He stood trembling by Becky, unable to speak.

'They're so highly strung,' she kept saying, to no animal in particular.

'Immature nitwits,' Reuben remarked, not caring who heard. 'I'd make them grow up!'

'What would you do, Reuben?' Asher asked eagerly.

'Leave them behind – make them fend for themselves.'

'Cruel beast,' retorted Becky.

'Cruel?' Reuben echoed. 'Cruel? Don't be absurd. They're young rams, not babies!'

Carl heard the altercation but went on his way; it was not for him to get mixed up in the disputes of sheep. He went straight toward the marshland, and unbeknown to him, Dancer followed. When Carl reached the place of his wallow, at first he could find nothing wrong. His small eyes flickered about, this way and that – he was short-sighted but his sense of smell was extremely powerful and he could smell sheep.

Prancer had ceased to bleat or struggle; with the fatalism of a dying animal he awaited death silently. Only his head protruded from the morass that had sucked him under. At last Carl saw him.

'Goodness, poor beast!' he grunted. 'Did you think yourself a hog? If you did, you didn't follow my footsteps.'

'Prancer!' called his brother. 'Are you alive?'

But there was no response from the trapped sheep.

'He is alive – just,' Carl remarked, turning at the sound of Dancer's call. 'But I don't know what we can do for him.'

'Save him, save him!' cried Dancer.

'Yes, yes. But how?'

'You got out again.'

'No, not at this point. There – look, there's where I had my wallow,' Carl indicated with his snout.

Prancer watched them with dull eyes, making no attempt to move.

'No,' Carl said in a low voice, 'I don't see there's anything I can do. It's really too late.'

Dancer, who could not keep still, ran off to his mother again. Carl looked at all that was visible of Prancer and Prancer gazed back blankly – the pig turned away, feeling awkward. A buzzard wheeled lazily above, its piercing gaze raking the ground; it missed nothing.

Becky saw the lamb return, still without his brother.

'Dancer, tell me,' she said firmly. 'Where is Prancer?'

'Stuck in the mud and Carl won't help,' he blurted out.

Jacob came over. 'Take us to him,' he said quickly. 'Why have you wasted time?'

Dancer led Becky and Jacob to the bog but Jacob saw at once that it was quite hopeless. In Frolic's case there had been a way out which she had taken herself; here there was none. The buzzard circled patiently, none of the animals aware of it.

Becky was horried. 'Oh no! Oh no!' she cried over and over. 'Dancer, how did this happen.'

'It was just a silly game,' Dancer wailed. 'It was so sudden.'

'I think they were trying to copy me,' Carl said, almost with an air of guilt.

'What stupidity!' Jacob exclaimed. 'Sheep pretending to be pigs! He'll lose his life for it.'

'Oh, don't say that,' Becky pleaded. 'Is there nothing—'

'Nothing,' Jacob interrupted with finality. 'Surely you can see for yourself?'

Becky became bitter in her despair. 'He's not your offspring. It's not Frolic or Jess this time, so the great Jacob turns his back!'

'Frolic freed herself in the end,' Jacob reminded the ewe. 'Don't put the blame for your youngster's stupidity on to me. You know if there was something I could do I would do it.'

'No, Barley was right,' Becky said sharply. 'Jacob has his favourites.'

Jacob stepped away, trying to retain his composure. Now Becky rounded on the pig.

'You're to blame for this!' she accused him. 'Bringing your weird habits before the eyes of these young ones. You led them into it!'

'No, no, you're mistaken, I—' Carl began.

'Leave her,' Jacob told him.

All this time Prancer kept silent; he did not even call to his mother. But now he had spotted the buzzard which had descended some metres for a closer look. He began to bleat in terror – a shrill, strident bleat which startled the other animals. Now they saw the buzzard themselves. Prancer began to struggle again, thrashing his trapped legs under the surface of the bog. His shoulders appeared above the ooze but he could make no real headway and he sank back again, exhausted.

'Oh, it's horrible!' cried Becky, beginning to edge forward on to the mark. Jacob saw her danger and butted her firmly on her side, knocking her back. Becky sprawled on the ground. 'It was the bird. I saw the bird,' she explained.

'We all saw it,' said Jacob. 'But it's no threat. It can't make a catch from a marsh!' But Jacob could give no comfort; with resignation he turned on his heel. Carl made himself scarce in another direction. Becky and Dancer lingered – neither of them could bear to desert the doomed young sheep.

Prancer suddenly called out, 'Dancer, mother, go! It's all up with me. I feel very weak; it won't be long now. Perhaps Reuben was right; I should have grown up earlier.'

A much sobered Dancer prepared to leave his brother – the lesson had not been lost on him. Their mother ewe still hesitated.

Jacob said nothing on his return to the flock. He lay down in exactly the same place as before and began to chew the cud, but the ewes looked at him and guessed he had failed. Dancer was the next to appear. Eventually Becky returned, slow of foot, with her head hanging low. She slumped to the ground with a great sigh.

A moment later she bleated, 'I couldn't bear it any longer. By now the marsh must have swallowed him.'

'And what of our intrepid leader?' muttered Barley. 'It seems he was content to come back unaccompanied this time.'

'Don't start on that again,' Myriam warned her.

Jacob regarded the ewes wearily. Then he spoke. 'Look, Barley,' he said to her, 'despite all your complaints, you've decided to remain with us. You're quite at leave to go where you will, as many of the others have done. There's no restraint upon you – but if you wish to continue as part of this flock, you must learn to be more sweet-tempered.'

'Thank you for the lecture, oh wise Jacob,' Barley replied sarcastically. 'You would, no doubt, like me to be your obedient little follower like the rest of them here. I'm afraid I'm not so easily impressed.'

'Then why do you stay?' he demanded. 'Of course I'm not perfect, whoever heard of such a ridiculous notion? But Barley, in the name of Sweetriver, why don't you just make your departure and leave me in peace?'

Barley fell silent; she did not want to wander the moorland alone. She did not really know what she wanted, but she resented the little clique of Jacob, Myriam, Frolic and now Jess. Becky tried to explain that Prancer had been beyond any beast's help, but Barley was not really interested in the fate of Prancer. She had always thought he and his giddy brother were of no account and, privately, she felt the dead lamb deserved his fate.

Bridget had chewed her way through the scene with her usual appearance of unconcern. She noticed everything nonetheless, and relished every word. She welcomed dissension, especially among the ewes. More than anything she wished for the downfall of Bell – Bell was usually quiet but Bridget knew her weakness and how she envied Myriam. Things might be very interesting when the tupping season arrived!

Carl went away to build himself up for the winter. In the forest, which was a small one, were some ancient beech and oak trees. With the satisfaction peculiar to a rooting pig, he munched his way through the banquet of beech mast and acorns that was spread in abundance amongst the leaf litter. Red squirrels eyed him suspiciously from pine branches; they regarded the autumn yield of nuts as their own. But Carl was oblivious of everything except what his snout found for him on the forest floor.

Towards dusk, while the Sweetriver flock was absorbed in grazing, Becky raised her head and gave a start of alarm. A strange dark shape was moving towards her through the gathering twilight. It was a beast with four legs; yet quite unlike any beast she could recognize. She gave a nervous, eerie sort of cry and backed away. The other sheep looked up sharply, they saw the creature too, and the ones near Becky tossed their heads uncertainly. Only one animal knew it for what it was: Dancer knew his twin brother and bleated with delight.

It was indeed the unfortunate Prancer, plastered from head to foot in mud and slime, returning from his marshy prison. Dancer's reaction brought the whole flock running around the young male who had been given up for lost. A chorus of sheep voices asked the same question – how had he escaped?

'Not by my efforts,' Prancer told them in a tremulous tone, his spirit completely crushed. 'A human came – from where I couldn't say – a young human. He saw me and risked his own life to pull me out. I jumped from his arms as he waded to safety and he did try to follow me, but I ran off – I was too quick for him.'

'Then humans do come up here?' Myriam voiced the thoughts of all of them.

'It was my luck that that one did,' Prancer muttered. Then his legs gave way and he rolled on to his back, too weak to right himself.

'Are they searching for us?' a number of ewes demanded of Jacob.

'I know no more than you,' he answered. 'It might well be so.'

Dancer and Becky were trying desperately to get Prancer to his feet. They pushed, nudged and butted at his slippery body, and he staggered to all fours and stood for a moment, his four legs shaking violently. Then he lay down again and began to crop the vegetation.

'Was the human one you had seen before?' Jacob asked him.

'No,' he answered, tearing voraciously at the nearest grass tufts.

'But there may be more of them,' Jacob said. 'What do you wish to do? Move on?' He was asking the whole flock for an answer.

'We should disperse,' said Reuben. 'They will find it more difficult to capture us singly or in pairs.'

'But they would mean us no harm, surely?' Bell queried. 'Would it be so bad to be pastured again under their care?'

'Care?' cried Reuben angrily. 'I've no wish for their sort of care – under the rule of a dog with no choice of where we want to go.'

'I feel it would be wrong to disperse altogether, Reuben,' Jacob told him. 'There are dangers up here that none of us have faced before. We have more chance in a flock.'

'More chance of being rounded up, yes,' said his determined son. 'You don't like the idea of losing your position of dominance,' he went on, 'that's all it is. We've heard about these dangers on and off – where are they? Show them to me!'

'Foolish animal,' Jacob admonished him. 'You know nothing – you've yet to have your coat cut for the first time. I tell you the winter weather is close. It will be your first winter – don't face it alone or persuade others to do so!'

'I'm more likely to survive than your old carcass,' Reuben retorted. 'I'll take my chances. I've no wish to be taken by the farmers. You think like the old animal you are, yearning for the comfort of a warm barn to keep out the draughts. I'll take the free cold air.'

'Hush, Reuben,' Myriam said gently. 'You're forgetting Jacob's years of wisdom; he thinks for the flock. And let's not be hasty – humans won't search in the dark even if they are searching for us at all. We have plenty of time to come to a decision.'

'Well, let each animal make its own decision,' said Reuben, a little more affably. 'Jacob can't decide for all of us.'

The ewes began to mumble and murmur amongst themselves, and they looked at Jacob and Myriam as if hoping for a lead. None of them voiced an opinion.

At length Jacob said, 'You all have the hours of darkness to think about what's best for yourselves. At dawn I'll go to look for signs of the humans. When we all know about their movements we can decide more easily.' He turned his steadfast gaze on Reuben.

'I can wait till then,' said his son. 'But I can tell you now – my ideas won't change.'

# —9—
# Reuben

Before daylight, rain began to fall heavily. The mud that had dried on Prancer's fleece became wet again and was washed off in thick brown drops that collected in a pool around him. Jacob waited for the sky to lighten. Myriam had told him during the night that, no matter what, she would stay with him and that that would mean most of the other ewes would too. It grew light, and the ram trotted away on his mission.

There was an unease in the flock. The cause of it was not entirely attributable to the possibility of human presence on the moors. Reuben had unsettled the sheep with his challenge to Jacob's authority. Some of them, especially the few young males, were inclined to side with him. Only Jess's loyalty remained unquestionably with Jacob. There was also an awareness of adulthood among the young sheep, the females included. Their maturity was all but attained and the tupping season, with all its strange new feelings, would soon be upon them. They waited for Jacob's return.

When he came back he announced that he had seen nothing – no movement at all in the empty landscape.

'The weather might keep them away for a time,' commented Reuben. 'I'm sure they're going to come. Prancer's experience will be related by his rescuer; it's only a matter of time.'

'You're very sure, it seems, of the movement of humans,' Jacob remarked wryly.

'It's as well to anticipate them,' Reuben said shrewdly. 'And I plan to get far away from this area.'

'Alone?' Myriam queried.

'That depends on the wishes of the others. I think I can count on at least one companion.'

'Asher – of course,' Jacob said.

'Yes, Asher – of course,' replied that young male defensively. 'Reuben and I see things alike.'

'I can only caution you again,' Jacob reiterated.

'We mean to be careful,' Reuben said. He looked around at the flock as if he felt he might be doing it for the last time. 'Come then, Asher.'

The two young rams wandered away without looking back.

'Reuben is almost the image of you,' Myriam remarked to Jacob. 'Look at the way he moves – the same sedate, elegant manner.'

'Thank you for the compliment, Myriam,' Jacob answered, with a barely perceptible twinkle in his brown eyes. 'I think his step may be a little more sprightly than mine!'

When the two were some distance away, they broke into a run and were soon lost from sight. Dancer and Prancer had watched them enviously. Their characters had been very much sobered by the experience of the marsh, but they were not sufficiently confident to break free from the influence of their elders. None of the other youngsters had Reuben's self-possession. But a yearning for independence was beginning to grow in the hearts of the males.

Rain, wind, sunshine and fog was the pattern of the weather as October gave way to November. When fog blanketed the moorland, the sheep stepped warily. Some of the barren ewes were separated from the flock since they spent longer grazing, while the others moved on and in time the main body of animals was reduced to about thirty. The last of the leaves were stripped by the wind from the few stunted rowans and hawthorns that dotted the surrounding country. Once the flock caught a glimpse of a portly Carl drinking from a pool, but he did not approach them.

The sheep ate well during the autumn, building up their reserves for the lean spell that would come. By the middle of November all the members of the flock were in their prime and ready for the urgent rituals of the tupping. Jacob felt a resurgence of his need to dominate – he regarded the ewes in the flock as his own and he intended to brook no rivals. Dancer, Prancer and the other young rams had begun to show an interest in the ewes for the first time and Jacob knew it was time to assert himself. Only Jess, who remained inseparable from Frolic, would he tolerate. Whenever one of the other males strayed too close to a ewe, Jacob got between them. And he was an imposing animal: he had put on weight; he was firm, muscular and full of the confidence of years and experience. The older ewes followed him as if he were a magnet and they began to look to secure a position of advantage over their companions. But the young females, who recently had reached their full development, were attracted by the high spirits of Jacob's juniors. Jacob began to hustle them to keep them in line.

Dancer was emboldened by the interest he had attracted in a rather quiet little ewe who was known as Snow because of the particular whiteness of her fleece. They tried frequently to get together but Jacob seemed to be always watchful and he always prevented it. Dancer found this more and more frustrating.

'I don't know why he can't let us alone,' he said to his brother. 'He wouldn't miss the company of just one of the ewes?'

Barley overheard. 'Jacob's harem, that's what we are,' she quipped. 'Or that's how he sees us. He is to have sole dominion over us all.'

'I don't like that,' said Dancer. 'Neither does my brother.'

'Your day will come,' Barley told him. 'Jacob is old.'

'Then he should give way,' remarked Dancer.

Barley chuckled. 'He's not that old,' she murmured.

Dancer persisted in his efforts to court Snow. He was not ready to challenge Jacob so he tried other manoeuvres; he always fed near the little ewe and tried to whisper suggestions to her about separating themselves from the flock. But Jacob only had to bend his brows and Dancer would instantly fall silent: he was easily intimidated. Then he tried to outwit Jacob by staying awake when the old ram appeared to sleep. But somehow Jacob seemed always to have one eye open for him – he was prepared for everything Dancer might try. The young ram's spirits flagged as all his endeavours came to nothing, and Snow began to lose her interest in him. But then events took a different turn.

In the middle of a cold blustery morning, Reuben reappeared. Jacob knew why he had come – there could only be one reason. Reuben came purposefully into the centre of the flock, and he stared at Jacob. His father stared back.

'We know each other, Jacob,' said Reuben quietly. Yet his voice betrayed a suppressed excitement.

'You should have kept your distance,' Jacob told him. 'It would have been wiser.'

'The time of Jacob is over,' Reuben continued. 'Now

mine has come.' His body was tense.

'My time is not over,' Jacob warned. 'Not until I know that it is so.'

'Then know it now,' Reuben said. His head began to lower almost imperceptibly.

Jacob looked at the strong young animal he had sired, and assessed Reuben's strength inwardly. His young limbs would certainly be more agile than his own; his muscular form would be powerful, but he doubted if Reuben could match him for stamina.

'You need not have sought me out, Reuben,' he said. 'You could have followed the ewes who strayed – there are many of them.'

'You have the pick of the flock,' Reuben told him. 'Why should I surrender that to you?'

'Surrender?' Jacob retorted angrily. 'You are arrogant, Reuben. You live in your dreams.'

'I'll show you otherwise,' said the young male.

'Maybe. But I think you'll discover you're challenging me too soon!'

Asher hovered nearby, almost breathless with anticipation. He was gripped by fear, excitement, the thrill of combat.

Suddenly Jacob relaxed. 'I'll make a concession,' he announced.

Reuben looked at him in surprise.

'Choose yourself a willing ewe,' Jacob offered. 'I grant you the freedom to choose from the flock. Then take her away – and your henchman too.' He spoke scornfully to Asher.

Asher was furious; he waited for Reuben's anger to kindle. But Reuben, to his amazement, began looking over the ewes. He was doing as he was bid!

'He's mocking you, Reuben. Can't you see?' Asher spluttered in exasperation.

Reuben ignored him. His eye had picked out Snow and he began to step slowly towards her. Snow pretended to be unaware and continued cropping the turf. But Dancer noticed with alarm, his ardour aroused by jealousy. For a moment his usual meekness was forgotten; he ran over and put himself in Reuben's path.

The sturdy young ram halted in disbelief at this presumption. Then, with no warning at all, he charged. Dancer was hurled out of the way and tumbled over and over, falling on his back amongst a group of the older ewes. Now Reuben's blood was up; he recalled his real purpose.

'No, Jacob,' he said. 'Your ploy won't work. I won't be diverted from my intention.'

'That being, I assume, to challenge me for leadership of the flock?' Jacob's voice was ironical. 'And you, scarcely full grown!'

Reuben was riled. His front feet scraped at the turf and he swung his head about. The tension in the flock made the air seem to vibrate but Jacob kept calm. He meant to make Reuben do something rash and then turn it to his own advantage. Asher was beside himself with frustration.

'Reuben, what are you waiting for?' his thin, shrill bleat rang out.

Reuben rounded on him, 'Be quiet!' he snapped. 'You're only good at standing on the sidelines, muttering. If you're not careful I will treat you the same way as Dancer!'

Asher was mortified. He moved farther off, feeling foolish in front of the young ewes.

'Why don't you yield gracefully, Jacob?' Reuben bleated. He was loath to launch an attack on his respected father.

'Yield?' cried Jacob. 'To an immature creature with his

first season's wool still on him? Just how many lambs
have you sired?'

Jacob's contemptuous barb really struck home.
Reuben's blood raced, 'Now you've gone too far,' he
bellowed, 'and you'll pay for it!'

He dropped his head and raced towards Jacob, but at
the last moment Jacob turned and butted Reuben a
glancing blow in his side. The young ram was unaffected,
he wheeled about and charged again. Again Jacob
avoided him easily. The other sheep moved away out of
the reach of the pair, giving them a wide berth. Reuben
tried the same tactics but, as long as he continued lowering his head in order to present his horns, he was unable
to see in which way Jacob would move. Jacob was quite
aware of this; he was content for Reuben to carry on in
this way until he exhausted himself. So the youngster
charged to and fro, his anger increasing with each of his
vain attempts to make contact. He began to breathe
heavily and at length he cried furiously, 'Is this how you
show your strength, Jacob?'

'In combat,' his father answered coolly, 'there is not
only bodily strength to be considered, but strength of
mind also.'

'Damn you!' roared Reuben. 'Why won't you meet me
head to head and settle it honourably?'

'You're very proud of your new young horns, I'm
sure,' Jacob returned. 'But mine have all the hardness of
age. They'd shatter yours at the first blow!'

The old ram was bluffing; if anything his horns were
the brittle ones after his many years. But he calculated
that the youngster would know nothing of this, and
Reuben was disconcerted.

He looked at Jacob for a long while, trying to read his
thoughts, but Jacob was inscrutable. Reuben suspected a
bluff, but dared not call it. Now he really felt at a loss – he

was too proud to back down.

Jacob guessed much of what was going through his offspring's mind and he decided to help Reuben to save face.

'My offer still stands,' he said. 'You won your ewe with ease – take her.'

Reuben was tempted; maybe he was too inexperienced to be the dominant ram just yet. 'All right,' he said, rather sullenly. 'But make no mistake, Jacob, this is not the end of it. You grow more ancient each day, and I shall be waiting.'

'I understand you,' said Jacob. He knew he had won – for now.

Reuben walked away and sought out Snow. With a little skip she was by his side, apparently eager to partner him and this time Dancer made no attempt to interfere. But there was still Asher. He seemed to think Reuben would still require his company – he soon discovered otherwise.

'Lose yourself, Asher,' Reuben told him harshly. 'Find some solitary old ewe and make yourself comfortable. When tupping is over, we may meet again.'

Asher was crestfallen. He was not ready to start life on his own; Reuben had always decided everything. He watched his hero stalk away with the pretty ewe, then he looked towards the main flock that had soon collected around Jacob again. With hesitant steps he began to walk towards them, stopping frequently as if dreading a rebuke. But none of the sheep, Jacob included, seemed to notice him. Asher felt terribly insignificant. Eventually he was absorbed into the flock again as if no animal cared that he had ever left or returned. He did not know whether to feel relieved or affronted.

Reuben wandered away, knowing that he had come off worse in the encounter. But an idea came to him which

retored some of his self-esteem. There were other ewes
on the moorland, as Jacob had said, under no ram's control – he could form his own flock. The demands of the
tupping season overrode every other consideration: he
had seen no humans, and his original idea of a flock
being more easily rounded up was temporarily forgotten.

'Where are we going, Reuben?' Snow asked him
quietly. She was actually a little frightened of him.

'To my territory,' he boasted. 'I rule there, and have no
rivals. My flock will be under my sway alone.'

'Flock? Sway?' repeated Snow. 'What am I to be
then?'

'You'll be my favourite,' Reuben assured her. 'I've
chosen you.'

Snow was quite pleased at this. 'But you have no flock?'
she asked in a puzzled way. 'There are only the two
of us.'

'Just for now, yes,' Reuben answered mysteriously. He
knew where some of the other separated ewes were, he
also knew that most of them were several seasons older
than he, and he wondered how they would react to him.
They might view his notion as impudent.

Reuben and Snow fed together near a little stream
which was stained brown by peat and drank their fill.
Then Reuben told Snow to stay put – he meant to begin
his search there and then.

'Stay here alone?' Snow bleated. 'I shouldn't like that;
I've never, ever been alone.' Her voice quavered.

'I shall not be gone long,' Reuben said. 'I'll bring company back for you.'

'Please be quick. I don't want to be alone in the dark,'
she said.

'I promise.'

Reuben trotted away, trying to look and feel confident.

He was proud of his appearance: he was fit and healthy and there was a springiness in his step – but he still had some misgivings about how he would deal with experienced ewes.

He came across a solitary female after a while, kneeling comfortably amongst some of the rusting bracken, whilst she ruminated. At the sight of Reuben she got up instantly and bleated, and Reuben knew at once the power of the male – he was exultant. The ewe followed him without a murmur and Snow had barely got used to being alone when Reuben returned. The three of them rested together.

The following days brought further additions to Reuben's flock, and it soon numbered about a dozen animals. He was very proud of his new position of eminence, and he began to dream of the day when he would unite these ewes with the ewes who still followed Jacob, making one large flock again. But first he would have to eliminate all the other males. His vanity made him believe that none of the young males of his own season could match him for strength, and he was probably right. But then there was Jacob. Still, after another winter his father's old body would be worn out, and then he would challenge him again.

The rituals of the tupping season now dominated the lives of all the Sweetriver sheep, and there promised to be many births in the Spring to enlarge the flock's population. But while the urgency of this period held the attention of all the animals, an ugly new menace to the sheep's safety suddenly appeared on the scene.

The first to be aware of it was Reuben. There were still many solitary ewes on the moorland; he had not rounded up every animal who had become separated from the original flock. And one day he came across one of these or, rather, the remains of her. The ewe had been killed and devoured by what must have been an enormous, fierce beast. Her throat had been torn out, and the killer had ripped the carcass to shreds, only the head was intact. Vestiges of the animal's fleece clung in tufts to the skin and bones that remained and dotted the surrounding vegetation. Reuben had been led to the discovery by the sight of a pair of ravens tearing at a large object on the ground and when he reached the spot he found the sheep unrecognizable as one of his former companions.

Reuben gazed at the horrible sight with revulsion and yet with a perverse fascination: he had never beheld such a thing before. What terrible creature could have done this? A grown ewe was a large animal, and no fox was powerful enough to make such a kill on its own. Reuben did not have sufficient experience to know the answer, but it was evident that something powerful and terrible was loose on the moors, and that meant that all the sheep were threatened.

He hastened to warn his females. 'We must all be extra vigilant,' he told them. 'We're all in danger, every one of us.'

'What can it be?' Snow bleated in fright.

'I don't know,' Reuben admitted.

'Jacob should be told. He must take precautions too,' one of the older ewes said.

'Yes.' Reuben agreed. 'I'd thought of it already. I'll go to him.'

The ewes were understandably nervous about being left alone now; they saw Reuben as their protector and Snow began to insist on going with him.

'Whatever beast it is, it wouldn't attack a whole group of sheep. You'd be better off staying here, Snow, with the others. I'm the one taking the risk of being attacked – by travelling alone.'

'Then don't go, Reuben,' she begged. 'We need you

here. Jacob will know what to do.'

'Not if he's unaware that the danger exists,' Reuben reminded her, 'and it's very likely he is. No, I'll go now whilst there is good light – and I shall go very cautiously, you may be sure.'

Snow knew there was no choice for him really, he could not allow any of the flock to remain in ignorance of such a threat. When Reuben was gone, the ewes bunched together tightly. Every slight noise made them tremble. A dozen times one or other of them thought she heard the panting breath of some unknown monster in the murmur of the wind, or the rustling of the long, dead stalks of grass. Hour after hour they teetered on the brink of panic, whilst Reuben made his way safely to the larger flock.

When Jacob saw him approaching he thought another challenge was about to be presented by his strong young son, and just managed to mask his surprise when Reuben at once blurted out his news.

'Yes,' he said in reply. 'We've known of this menace a little longer than you, and have already lost one of our number. It happened at night, the beast pulled one of the ewes down whilst she was drinking and dragged her away. We heard nothing; saw nothing. But then in the daylight . . . .' He left the rest unsaid.

'What can we do, Jacob?' Reuben bleated.

'Nothing, except keep watch.'

'But how? We have to sleep.'

'Not all at the same time,' Jacob replied.

'Of course. But Jacob, what sort of animal is it?'

'A dog. It's Kep.'

'But that's impossible.'

'Of course it isn't impossible,' Jacob argued. He knew nothing of the collie's reunion with the master. 'Sheep are fair game even to a sheepdog when she's starving.'

Reuben was astounded. 'No, no,' he muttered in utter

bewilderment, 'it can't be her. She's smaller than a full-grown sheep. She hasn't the strength.'

Now Jess spoke up. 'She tried to kill me when I sought her help for Frolic,' he reminded Reuben. 'She would have had both of us if she could. But Jacob was there and he's too strong for her.'

'You and Frolic were still lambs then,' Reuben said. 'How could Kep slay a grown ewe? I thought it might be foxes.'

'Foxes hunt alone or in pairs,' Jacob told him. 'A ewe could deal comfortably with even two foxes.'

'Was your ewe weak?'

'No – far from it. A stout, heavy old thing. Have you left Snow alone?' Jacob asked sharply, as a thought suddenly struck him.

'Of course not,' Reuben answered indignantly. 'There are several other ewes in my flock now.'

'I see.' Jacob was almost amused. He understood at once that Reuben was proud of his achievement. 'Well, you must explain to them. Kep has turned sheep killer.'

# —10—
# Envy

During the tupping, Jacob was the cause of much envy and rivalry amongst the females. Bell saw this as her best chance of ousting Myriam from her position as favourite. She made herself as agreeable as she could to Jacob, who was well aware of her charms and kept with her more than any other ewe. Barley, too, enjoyed Jacob's favour at this time and many of the fat ewes who had not borne lambs in the spring, such as Bridget, were granted another chance of motherhood. But Myriam, old as she was, retained her special link with Jacob. He never overlooked her, they were old companions and no other ewe, however appealing, was able to destroy Myriam's unique relationship with Jacob. For a time, Bell was sure she had done so. She gloried in Jacob's attachment to her, but when he eventually left her again for Myriam's side she became sour and spiteful.

'Perhaps Reuben was right,' she said to Becky. 'Jacob must be near his dotage if he can prefer that grizzled old husk to the likes of us.'

'I think he sees Myriam as his deputy,' Becky answered, 'but I agree with you about Jacob. He must have had his last fling.'

'But he is such a fine ram,' Bell said wistfully. 'I wish Myriam wouldn't monopolize him so.' Really she still thought Jacob was marvellous. 'I can't bear to watch the way she slights all the other ewes.'

Bell was talking nonsense, borne of her bitter envy; Myriam never spoke a sharp word to any other sheep, and she did her best to be friendly and kindly to all. But Bell, Becky and another ewe who was also jealous of Myriam kept at a distance from the rest of the flock, where they indulged their complaints freely. They were sometimes joined by Bridget, who did not like Bell at all, and always did her best to exacerbate her envy. It was because of Bell and Becky keeping aloof from the others that the third ewe in their company lost her life . . . .

At night the three of them moved a little closer to the rest of the flock from the desire for safety. On the night of the killing, Bell and Becky left their companion drinking, expecting her to catch them up shortly, but she never got the chance. The killer, unknown to any of them, had been prowling around, waiting for just such an opportunity. It pulled the ewe down so swiftly that she was not able to utter a sound.

After this episode Bell and Becky learnt their lesson and mingled with the flock again. But Bell could not overcome her unhappiness. She started to harbour all sorts of unpleasant ideas about Myriam: with a killer dog on the loose no sheep was entirely safe and she wondered if there was some way in which Myriam might be exposed to danger. At the time Reuben came with news of a second killing, Bell was secretly trying to think of a plan that would rid the flock of the presence of Myriam for ever.

Dusk was just beginning to fall when Reuben prepared to return to his own ewes, and Bell thought she might be able to work something out of the situation. 'It's growing dark, Reuben,' she bleated to him. 'Why don't you stay here safely with us, until the morning? This killer dog seems to hunt at night.'

'No, I can't leave the others,' Reuben said at once. 'I'll be safe enough. The light will hold a bit longer yet; but thank you, Bell, for your concern.'

'Jacob, you mustn't let him go alone like this. He's so young, and the dog so cunning,' Bell kept on.

Reuben was not greatly flattered by this. 'Yes, I'm young,' he admitted. 'But I'm strong enough to deal with a dog of Kep's size.'

'You don't know her sly ways,' Bell insisted. 'She's so noiseless – none of us heard a sound of the last killing. She could drag you down from behind, before you would know she was there.'

Jacob was listening in considerable puzzlement; Bell had never shown such interest in Reuben before. Did she have a hankering for him? If that were so, Reuben must be got away at all costs. He had no intention of encouraging a liaison between them.

'Reuben will manage, Bell,' he said. 'We mustn't detain him any longer.'

'Well, he mustn't go by himself,' declared Bell. 'You'll go with him, won't you, Jacob?'

'How can I leave the flock?' Jacob demanded. 'I don't know what's got into you. You've never shown—'

Reuben broke in indignantly. 'This is all nonsense,' he said. 'I don't need Jacob's protection any longer. I've done well enough on my own, and I've got animals waiting who depend on me.'

'Then I will accompany you,' Bell announced. 'I have no defence against fierce carnivores, but two sheep together are more secure than one.' She seemed quite determined.

'Wait!' cried Myriam. 'If anyone goes, it should be me. I'm his mother.'

Reuben could not understand what was going on at all; Jacob had misinterpreted Bell's motives; only old

Bridget, shrewd in the ways of ewes, had an inkling of what the scene was all about.

Bell said, 'I suppose, Myriam, that would be more fitting.' She accepted Myriam's proposition with alacrity, pleased with the way her plan seemed to be working. Bridget's suspicions were confirmed and she saw her way clear to discredit Bell – but she waited a little.

'Myriam, Myriam,' said Jacob. 'What could you do that Reuben couldn't do himself? He's a ram now.'

'I can make two beasts instead of one – that's all,' Myriam replied. 'And it's true, a pair of sheep is less likely to be attacked.'

'But why should you risk yourself?' Jacob asked with concern.

'How can I let Bell go with him? She has no blood tie with Reuben.'

'If you must come, then come,' Reuben said impatiently. 'The whole thing is absurd. I'll be delayed no longer!' And he turned his back on the flock, his head full of images of Snow, slain in his absence.

Myriam went after him hesitantly. She was not quite sure why she suddenly found herself playing this unexpected role. But Bell was delighted with her success so far – Myriam had gone. The best of it was that the old ewe would probably try to make her way back to Jacob and the flock alone, either at dawn or, better still, during the night – such was her loyalty to the ram. And then she really would be laying her life on the line.

Bridget waddled across to Bell. 'A neat bit of work,' she muttered to her. Bell looked taken aback – then, quite slowly and deliberately, Bridget wandered across to Jacob who was still peering through the gathering evening after Myriam.

Bell watched with some alarm. She realized Bridget had seen through her.

'Jacob,' said Bridget, chewing for a while and assuming a pensive expression. 'You realize that that pretty innocent-looking little ewe has engineered all this?'

'What?' said Jacob. 'What do you say?' He was genuinely puzzled.

'I say Bell has deliberately sought to rid you of Myriam,' Bridget continued coolly. 'She wants your favour. She wants it all to herself.'

'What? How can you—? Are you telling me—?' spluttered Jacob. 'Bell!' he thundered.

She looked up meekly, afraid of his wrath.

'Oh yes, I see it all now,' Jacob muttered to himself. 'Bell, if you're planning treachery, you'll pay the price for it.'

'I only thought . . . .' she stammered.

'I see what you thought,' Jacob said, a hard edge to his voice. 'I tell you this, Bell. If Myriam doesn't return safe to this flock, I'll make you an outcast.'

Bell quaked before Jacob's anger, but Bridget gloated. She had waited a long time for this.

Meanwhile, Reuben and Myriam were silently crossing the moors, listening for the slightest suspicious noise. Neither spoke to the other: Myriam was puzzling over Bell's behaviour; Reuben was thinking of Kep. The more he thought about her, the stronger his conviction became that Jacob was wrong. Kep might have lost her master and turned hunter to survive, but she was not a big dog and Reuben found it difficult to picture her killing an adult ewe. And if the killer were not Kep, nor foxes, what could it be? None of them knew what other animals were roaming Leckmoor. Reuben was roused from his thoughts by the faint sound of bleating ahead of them, which soon grew into a chorus. They were frightened bleats, and Reuben knew immediately what was their source.

'Quickly, Myriam,' he said. 'There must be another attack!'

'Don't wait for me,' answered the old ewe. 'You go on – they're calling for you!'

With just a moment's hesitation, Reuben left her and hurried on toward his ewes.

As he neared them the noise became one of terror, and then a great bark shook the air. Reuben turned cold with fear, he had never heard such a bark before. But he kept running.

Suddenly a huge figure exploded out of the gloom and bounded past Reuben at a distance of only a few metres. It was a great black dog with a heavy muscular body, a broad head and huge jaws. It ran so fast Reuben caught only a glimpse of it, but he knew beyond any doubt now what was killing the sheep. The size of its gaping, hungry jaws with its exposed fangs told him everything.

The ewes pressed around him, panic-stricken; quaking and bleating in chorus. It was a long time before he could quieten them. They had been lucky; they had managed to drive the dog away, working together instinctively to prevent it from singling out one of their number to pull down. In the end it had run off to search elsewhere for its prey. But the ewes had not all escaped unscathed. Several of them had been nipped on the legs during the scruffle. Another one had the marks of the beast's fangs on her rump; she was bleeding profusely. All at once Reuben stood stock still. Myriam – she was alone and right in the path of the killer! His heart sank; there was nothing to be done. He felt he had sacrificed her, his own mother ewe!

'Oh, Myriam, Myriam,' he moaned, remorsefully.

The ewes looked at each other questioningly, knowing nothing of Bell's wicked manoeuvre.

Reuben waited for the horrible cries that would signify

Myriam's death, but there were none – only the most sinister kind of quiet. Then Reuben remembered the cunning and silence of the dog's kills before; its lone victims had known nothing of their attacker, and now, Myriam had given her life for him. Reuben stepped away from the other sheep – he wanted to be alone in his misery. The vision of the dog's gleaming fangs haunted his memory and he stared blankly into the darkness beyond.

All at once, he saw the familiar, grizzled figure of the old ewe coming towards him, running. Miraculously, Myriam had survived.

As soon as he was quite sure it was her, Reuben ran forward and nuzzled her, butting her playfully with delight. It was so unusual for Reuben to give any token of his feeling that Myriam was quite overcome.

'Oh Myriam, I was certain you had been killed,' Reuben told her. 'Did you see that great brute?'

'Yes, I saw him,' said Myriam. 'He ran right past me. I know the animal, and he knows me.'

Reuben was astounded. 'He ran past!' he repeated in wonder. 'But—'

'I've known him since he was a puppy,' she explained. 'He used to come to the farm with his master, who was a friend of our master. Jacob and myself both know the dog, he is a Rottweiler called Roger. He must have become homeless like Kep and I'm sure he recognized me.'

'Is that why you escaped – because he remembered you?'

'Maybe. Or, maybe he's not the killer.'

'There's no question of that. Ask the other ewes,' said Reuben.

'But what of Kep?' murmured Myriam.

'Come with me,' was Reuben's reply. He led her to the

injured ewe. 'Could Kep have done that?'

'No,' Myriam acknowledged. 'These are the marks of a more powerful beast.'

The ewes hastened to tell her of their experience; all talking at once, and all of them exaggerating the ferocity and size of the killer.

'Yes, yes,' said Myriam. 'You've all been lucky. I think we're safe as long as we stay in a group. The dog can't fight all of us.'

'Myriam, you must stay with us now,' said Snow.

'For a time, yes,' Myriam answered, 'while the dog hunts elsewhere.' She began to lick at the injured ewe's wounds, trying to staunch the blood.

Later Reuben said to Myriam, 'If this Roger has turned wild, could there be other abandoned dogs running loose up here?'

'Reuben, don't fret yourself unnecessarily,' she answered. 'Why fear the worst? We know how to evade the Rottweiler – numbers – the greater the number of sheep the less likely the attack . . . .'

Reuben pondered this, realizing what Myriam was hinting at. But he was not sure he wanted to rejoin Jacob and become an inferior again, even though tupping was over for the season.

'I do understand,' he said. 'But I've come to value my independence.'

'It's natural. But, Reuben, don't be too proud and live to regret it.'

The next morning Myriam returned safely to Jacob's side.

# —11—
# Sheep Killer

For a time Reuben held out, but December arrived and the temperatures crashed. Then the first snow fell; a few centimetres at first, giving warning of what was to come. Jacob was reminded of the pony's words, and the existence of dogs was forgotten as the problems of the season grew more severe. Reuben and his ewes became a little less vigilant as they wandered further afield to find sufficient to eat. The importance of food filled their minds.

One bright, moonlit night the Rottweiler returned, emboldened by hunger. The rabbits he had come to rely on were thin on the ground, and he was competing with hawks, foxes and owls for this food source. He recalled the flavour of raw mutton and with surprising swiftness he appeared, as if from nowhere, his eyes glowing in the moonlight. He killed the nearest ewe and dragged her off, vanishing as suddenly as he had come.

This incident caused Reuben to think very hard and he decided to consult Snow and the other ewes to see how they felt. They had been badly scared by the recent killing.

'What defence have we against this creature?' they asked Reuben, obviously feeling extremely vulnerable.

'We must all be more watchful,' he replied. 'Watch out for each other as well as ourselves. Remember, you drove the dog away once before.'

'Perhaps he wasn't so desperate then,' said Snow.

'Desperate enough,' said the ewe who had been injured. 'I still carry the scars.'

'Well then,' said Reuben, 'we have a choice. We can rejoin the main flock if you wish.'

Most of them seemed to like that idea and one of them remarked, 'Jacob is very wise: he must know how to deal with this menace.'

Reuben realized there was good sense in the ewe's remark, as much as he disliked hearing it. The decision appeared to have been taken.

'I'll lead you to the flock tomorrow,' he told them. 'We won't have any trouble before then; the dog must have eaten enough to last it for days.'

Some of the ewes shuddered at the picture Reuben's words conjured up of the Rottweiler gorging itself on one of their companions. They had seen the brute and could easily imagine the dog's great jaws tearing at her flesh. Instinctively, they huddled closer together; the little flock resembling one huge animal with many heads.

More snow fell at night. It was very cold but the sheep, whose fleeces had grown thick again, were better protected than any other creature on the moors against the rigours of temperature. Their white bodies gave them almost perfect camouflage against the winter landscape, and it was this that helped to protect them from recapture; for humans were out looking for them in the National Park.

Word had been passed here and there amongst those who lived around Leckmoor, originating from the walker who had discovered Prancer and rescued him. This person had seen one lone sheep and had commented on it to a friend. Gradually over the weeks the idea grew that sheep were likely to be wandering the moorland and, with the onset of the hard weather, some interested local people had banded together to mount a search. These people were not from Sweetriver, so the connection between Talbot and his lost flock was not made. For his part, Talbot had long ago given up any idea that his sheep had survived the flood.

It chanced to be Reuben who became aware of the humans' approach first – he heard men's voices in the distance and rose to his feet. Some fifty metres or so away, he saw two men and a dog. Luckily the sheep were sheltering behind a screen of stunted thorn to escape the worst of the wind, and were not spotted. He quickly alerted the ewes and led them at a run over the snow away from the searchers. Then they were seen and human cries rang in the crisp air. The dog was commanded to chase them, and Reuben and his flock were made to flee from their canine pursuer.

Reuben led them down an incline, and for a while the dog lost them from view. The young ram headed for the fringe of the forest which was only half a kilometre distant and the ewes ran behind him without a sound, fear lending them additional speed. They passed the first pine trees and ran on into the forest gloom; the darkness of the place seemed to swallow them up and they hid themselves among the cluster of huge tree trunks which grew straight and tall. The canopy of foliage had let in little of the snow, but the boughs were weighed down with it, and the steady, soft drops of lumps of snow falling to the ground was the only sound that disturbed the forest's silence. The sheep's breath steamed in the cold air and spiralled upwards to the branches above.

The dog had lost them and more snow was falling to cover their trail. Reuben hoped they were secure.

'Now Jacob's in danger,' he said. 'A larger flock will be easier to detect – but we must bide here for a while before we try to discover their whereabouts.'

The ewes began looking around for something to nibble at, remarking to each other on the scarcity of any promising vegetation, and their bleats were overheard by an animal who had taken up residence in the forest and came now to investigate. They looked up to see their old acquaintance, Carl, come lumbering toward them. 'Well, well,' he grunted. 'I thought we should meet again.'

He was fatter than the sheep remembered, but his eyes roved restlessly around as if he were not quite sure of himself.

'The joke's on me now, isn't it?' he chuckled. 'I'm the one feeling discomfort these days; I just don't know how to get out of this cold. I've done the best I could – made a sort of litter of leaves and bracken and such like – but it doesn't seem to make a lot of difference.'

Reuben realized the pig had been suffering and was trying to appear cheerful. 'Has it been very bad for you?'

'Pretty bad, yes,' Carl admitted. 'It's worst in the dark hours. I sometimes go to sleep and dream that I am freezing to death in the night.'

'Poor old Carl,' said Snow. 'I thought your hide was very thick?'

'So it is, but what I'd give for a nice warm woolly covering . . . .'

'What can we do to help you?' Reuben asked. 'We'd certainly like to if we can. It must be real misery for you.'

'Misery? Yes, that's a good description. But, wait a bit . . .' Carl was looking about him, 'there were more of you. Where are the others?'

Reuben answered. 'We don't all roam together these days, although until I saw the humans just now, we were on the point of rejoining the others.'

'Humans?' Carl grunted, looking suddenly much more alert. 'Where are they? Nearby?'

'I hope not,' said Reuben. 'I hoped we had escaped them.'

'I hope they are,' admitted Carl. 'It's my only chance now. I would love to be rescued and taken to a nice warm sty with plenty of dry straw in it; these days I'm always cold and wet.'

'If you leave the forest you might run into them,' Reuben said helpfully. 'But please – keep them away from us.'

'Of course,' Carl muttered. 'I'll leave you then. Oh, warmth, warmth!' he grunted as he hastily trotted off.

The ewes stared after him. 'Are you sure we're doing the right thing hiding in here?' one of them asked Reuben after a while. 'There's a lot to be said for warmth and shelter in the winter.'

Reuben, who, of course, had yet to experience the duration of a winter, was puzzled. 'You're forgetting the dog,' he reminded her.

The ewe fell silent. After a long interval a rather downcast Carl was seen returning to join them. It seemed the pig had been unlucky. 'No trace of them as far as I could see,' he announced morosely. 'I'm off to my litter, but first, you didn't explain how you sheep have become separated?'

'Simple enough,' said Reuben. 'Males don't get on in the mating season.'

'I follow you,' said Carl. 'What are your plans then?'

'To return to the flock,' Reuben said. 'There's a killer dog about and a small group like us is too much at risk. But now we're caught between two threats. The humans will be looking for a large flock, and they might have parties all over the moors.'

'I see. And you want to stay free?'

'Of course,' said Reuben. 'Humans are partnered by dogs and we've learnt enough about dogs never to want to associate with them again.' He went on to describe their experiences with the Rottweiler, telling the pig just how savage and bold the dog was.

Carl looked perturbed. 'This is bad news,' he said. 'After all I must be fair game, too, for this creature.'

'I hadn't thought of that,' Reuben answered. 'But it is a very strong animal.'

'I shall have to watch out,' said the pig. 'Does the dog come into the forest? My litter's rather noticeable.'

'I couldn't tell you,' Reuben admitted. 'But as long as sheep stay in the open I imagine we're easier prey, and we have to stay out to find food to feed the flock.'

'It's a pity,' said Carl. 'It gets very lonely in here,' and he wandered off, back to his litter.

'Come on,' said the young ram to his ewes. 'The way must be clear now. We should complete our journey so at least we can warn the others about the men.'

They left the shelter of the trees. Snowflakes were falling thickly now, making their discovery by the men less likely, and Reuben led them towards the place where he remembered Jacob and his flock had last gathered. It was a difficult journey: visibility was poor and, as the snow deepened, their progress was slowed down.

'Are you sure we're on the right track?' one of the ewes asked. The journey seemed to go on for ever.

'No, I'm not sure,' Reuben had to say. 'I only hope—' He broke off as some dark shapes loomed into sight a few metres away – it was a group of ponies, standing by a frozen pool as they stolidly munched mouthfuls of vegetation. They had scraped a hole in the snow with their hooves to reach the lichen, dead grass and dry stalks underneath, quite at home with this sort of diet, even enjoying it.

Reuben stopped by them. 'Have you seen others of our kind in the region?' he asked. 'We're in danger of losing our way.'

One of the ponies turned his dark, long-lashed eyes on the ram and regarded him without interest, 'I have seen other sheep,' hc said. 'You've been around here since the summer, haven't you?'

'Yes, but I was asking if you had seen them recently,' Reuben explained.

'Yes, there was a large number of sheep around,' one of the other ponies observed, 'with an old male. I saw them recently; they can't be far away.'

'Oh, thank goodness,' Reuben said with some relief. 'Thanks for your help.'

The sheep continued on their way and they started to bleat now, hoping their calls might reach their old companions. After a while they heard an answering bleat and they hurried on. Presently they saw movement ahead; the first animal they came across was Asher who seemed to be on his own. He was overjoyed to see Reuben again, and poured forth a flood of questions.

'Wait, wait!' cried Reuben. 'Where are the others? You're not alone, surely?'

'No, they're around,' Asher answered him. 'But, I've no particular friend in the flock nowadays and so I keep myself to myself.'

Reuben was sorry for his friend, but he warned him at once, 'Don't you know the risks you're running with that sheep-killer on the prowl?'

'I keep my eyes open; you needn't concern yourself,' Asher replied rather sullenly.

'But I do concern myself. If you saw the beast, what could you do?'

'Run,' replied Asher, with hollow amusement in his voice. 'Anyway, you haven't told me your reason for coming this way.'

'The dog. As Myriam said, "safety in numbers".'

As they went along he quickly described to Asher their escape from the humans, and how they had encountered Carl in the forest.

'That sounds like the answer to our problems – the forest,' Asher remarked. 'If only we could solve the food problem.'

'I agree,' said Reuben. 'I'll discuss it with Jacob.'

And even as he spoke he saw the old ram, standing at the top of a slight rise in the ground and looking in their direction, just as if he had been waiting for them. He seemed such a solid and dependable figure that even Reuben took comfort from the sight of him.

'Well, well,' Jacob began, 'I thought I heard you. And all your little collection of ewes, too! What brings you here?'

Reuben enlightened him at once.

'Humans out looking?' Jacob repeated. 'Not for long in this weather, I shouldn't think.'

'You think they'll disperse?'

'Bound to. They'll be wanting shelter too,' Jacob declared.

'Good. Then that might settle things as far as we're concerned,' said Reuben. 'We think one large flock is the safest measure for all of us whilst the sheep killer is around.'

'Of course it is,' agreed Jacob. 'I'm so glad you feel that way. And don't think, Reuben, I shall be wanting to inter-fere with your sphere of influence. You take my meaning?'

Asher thought he was being totally overlooked, as usual. 'I'm a ram too,' he said. 'Why am I disregarded in this way. It's insulting. First Jacob, now Reuben; why do you settle everything? And what about Dancer and Prancer; we're all grown rams now.'

'It's a question of authority,' Reuben explained. 'Jacob is the wisest of us and I've earned the right to be regarded as a leader in my own small way. And Asher, if you remember, you used to follow me around and—'

'I was young and naive then,' Asher muttered. 'You were the biggest and the eldest of the lambs, so it was natural – but now it's different. Do you see now why I keep my own company? I'm tired of being snubbed.'

They were amongst the rest of the flock now and some of the ewes turned to Asher as they heard these remarks, gazing at him curiously. But he avoided their stares and went off to be alone again.

After the mutual greetings between the large and the small flock, Reuben felt sorry for the way he had spoken to his friend. There had been a time when Asher would have taken his side against any animal -- even Jacob. He sought his old companion out deliberately. 'I'm sorry,' he said. 'Of course you must be consulted; and I think you're right, the forest is the answer to our difficulties – at least for a while. Let's be friends again, just like we used to be but on an equal basis now.'

Asher was delighted; his chest seemed to swell with this remark, 'I ask nothing more,' he murmured.

Jacob, Reuben, Asher and Myriam now discussed their tactics. They talked about Carl's offer to help look for food, and of how long it would be before the cunning Roger would be back to claim another victim. It did not take them long to agree that shelter in the winter weather was something they needed urgently.

So the Sweetriver flock was united again. Some solitary individuals remained on the moorland: those whom Reuben had not found during the tupping, but the rest of

the flock grazed methodically together in the relentless
snow, before setting off hopefully for the protection of
the forest. As always, Jacob led and Myriam followed
close behind with Jess and Frolic. Then came the bulk of
the ewes who had stayed with Jacob, together with Prancer
and Dancer, Becky and Barley. Since her disgrace, Bell
had been ostracized by most of the flock. She walked
near Becky who sometimes spoke to her; but Bridget,
Bell's triumphant enemy, kept as far away from her as she
could at all times now. She suspected that Bell planned
revenge.

Myriam and Jacob despised both of these ewes, both
contemptible in their different ways. At the rear of the
flock were Snow and Reuben's other ewes, and at the very
back, Reuben himself and Asher, keeping a constant
look-out for danger.

So the flock moved along, battling against the gusts of
wind which dashed stinging flurries of snow against their
bowed heads.

'Carl will be glad to see us,' Reuben remarked to
Asher. 'He wanted us to join him.'

As the sheep neared the edge of the forest, suddenly
there was a scramble of movement on the right flank of
the flock. Jacob was unaware of anything wrong but
Reuben suspected the worst. The ewes began bleating
and some of them reared up and dashed away in their
fright. A horrible bark and a strangled cry told Reuben
his suspicions were correct: the sheep killer, who had
been silently tracking the flock's progress, had returned
and killed again. With its usual speed the Rottweiler had
dragged the victim off almost before it had been noticed
and only a thick trail of blood in the snow was left as
evidence.

Jacob halted now and came round to investigate.
Reuben met him, grim-faced, 'This brute Roger is killing

for the enjoyment of it,' he said. 'Not for food.'

'I feared it might come to this,' answered Jacob. 'A dog turned killer in this way sometimes gets a lust for blood; then it will return and kill again and again. We shan't be safe even in the forest.'

'No,' Reuben agreed, 'particularly as it must know our destination. It must have been shadowing us all along.'

Myriam was trying to soothe the terrified ewes and bring them all back into a group. It was a difficult task and it was quite a while before the identity of the victim was discovered. The killer had struck at one of the older, fatter ewes. The dog's strength was tremendous.

The flock hastened to get into the depths of the forest; some of them running blindly, stumbling over each other and almost causing a stampede. Only Jacob's bellows of authority quietened them and gradually a semblance of order returned. The snow no longer stung their faces and the sheep felt a little comforted.

Jacob said to Myriam, 'We have got to rid ourselves of this menace. It could kill us all.'

'Roger passed me by,' Myriam said. 'He remembered me from long ago and he must also recognize you. Can we reason with him, do you think?'

'The dog's beyond reason now,' Jacob answered. 'He's become like a mad creature. Can you picture him stopping still to listen to our pleas? No, Myriam, something much more drastic is called for.'

'I can think of nothing,' she said.

'I'll talk to Reuben,' Jacob murmured. He was beginning to value his son's opinion.

But Reuben had no suggestions to make. 'What can sheep do against such savagery?' was his comment, and he and Jacob stood listening to the wind roaring in the pine tops.

'Well, we could mount a guard,' Jacob said eventually. 'You and me alternately – and perhaps Asher,' he added as an afterthought. 'It's the suddenness of the killings that is so awful; if we were prepared, had some warning . . . .'

'We can give it a try,' answered Reuben.

'Somehow,' said Jacob, 'we've got to prevent this terrible dog from killing again, even if it means turning killers ourselves.'

# —12—
# The Lure

It was not long before Carl heard the noise of the sheep, and he rose hurriedly from his litter to go and greet them. He was delighted to see the whole flock present, and asked Jacob hopefully, 'Will you be staying?'

'We'll be staying until it's safe to leave again,' Jacob answered.

Carl was not sure if the ram was referring to the cruel weather or to the Rottweiler. 'Any sign of that terrible dog again?' he asked timidly.

'The brute killed one of us on our way here,' Jacob told him, 'and it knows where to find us now. This forest can be no sanctuary for us while the dog roams unchecked.'

Carl looked really alarmed. 'Another death?' he gasped. The pig's little eyes roved around, as if he expected to see the dog at that moment creeping through the trees. 'We're none of us secure then,' he continued, his fear making him show his resentment, 'and now you've almost led the killer here to pick us off as it chooses?'

'Of course we didn't lead it here,' Jacob said angrily. 'Don't you know how a dog can track its quarry? It followed our trail without our knowing anything about it, then it killed and departed as swiftly as it had come. We were quite helpless.'

'We must put our heads together,' said Carl, 'or we won't survive.'

'Reuben and myself are going to keep a constant watch for the beast's return,' said Jacob. 'Have you any suggestions to make?'

'Give me a chance,' the pig grunted. 'But I don't understand,' he added. 'Is the dog stocking its own larder? Surely it can't need such vast quantities of food, just for itself?'

'Reuben and I believe it has begun to kill just for sport,' Jacob answered. 'And that makes it a much more dangerous adversary.'

'Yes, we must act,' Carl said purposefully. 'We can't simply cower under the pine trees. Give me a while, there might be something we can do together. You're a large animal and I'm not exactly underweight!' He began to head back to his bed of bracken. Then a thought struck him, and he grunted and wheeled about, 'By the way,' he said, 'we have another companion in our forest refuge. I came across a solitary cat earlier who is looking for shelter here.'

'What sort of cat?' Jacob asked. 'Black and brown?'

'Yes, how did you know?'

'We saw it many days ago. But I'm glad you told me; cats are shrewd animals and it might be of use to us.'

'Indeed? Well, I'll try to find it again. It's probably up a tree somewhere.' Carl trotted off.

The sheep busied themselves searching the forest floor for whatever nourishment they could find. Jacob stood alone, a short distance from the flock, looking and listening for the enemy. All was peaceful enough as more snow filtered through the pine branches.

Reuben eventually came to join his father. 'See if you have any luck finding food,' he said ironically. 'My turn to keep the flock safe!'

'There's not much to be found, I know,' said Jacob. 'We're going to have to learn to enjoy the taste of moss and fungus, at least for a while.'

Towards evening Carl returned, bringing with him the tabby cat, who regarded the flock of sheep with the typically disdainful expression of its kind.

'We saw you on the moors before the snow fell,' Jacob said to the newcomer.

The cat did not reply. It looked at Jacob with its compelling green eyes and then yawned elaborately – almost contemptuously.

'The cat's called Francis,' said Carl. 'He knows all about the dog: it chased him.'

'How did you escape? It's so fast,' asked Snow.

'I ran up a tree, of course,' Francis answered bluntly. 'An escape route denied to animals such as you.'

'Francis thinks he has an idea for ridding us of the threat,' Carl explained. 'But there is one very large problem with it.'

'Any idea is most welcome,' Jacob remarked enthusiastically. 'Please tell us what it is.'

'Of course. I didn't come all this way in the company of a very smelly pig to sit here silent,' the tabby cat answered rudely.

Carl grunted with amusement. He did not consider this an insult; he enjoyed strong smells.

'I presume you're the head of this gathering of wool and mutton?' Francis remarked to Jacob.

'Yes,' answered the ram, taken aback by the unusual tone of this small animal. He tried to assume his most dignified demeanour.

'Good, well step aside over here, with the pig. Don't want everyone in on the plan at this stage – it might cause a bit of panic amongst those who haven't the sense to appreciate it.'

'Reuben here must join us,' Jacob replied at one. 'And Myriam too. It's equally necessary for them to hear.'

'Are you sure that's all?' Francis asked sarcastically.

'Yes, yes, quite sure,' Jacob bleated, looking at Reuben in slight dismay.

The cat moved away in his nonchalant manner and took up a position under a particularly large tree. When he realized that he would be dwarfed by the three sheep and the pig if he remained on the ground, he quickly ran up the tree trunk to the lowest branch and settled himself on that.

'Now listen,' he began. 'We all know the Rottweiler will be back, and we also know that none of us can rest easily as long as that thought is in our heads. So the dog has got to be disposed of – and I mean for good.'

'Yes,' agreed Jacob. 'We had already come to that conclusion.'

'Well, your horns are the weapons best suited for the job,' Francis continued. 'Between you, the dog wouldn't stand a chance.'

'But it's such a fierce beast; its great jaws could tear us in shreds,' said Reuben doubtfully.

'Then obviously you wouldn't let it get anywhere near enough to do so,' the cat replied impatiently. 'That huge weight of bone you carry on your heads could crush the dog before it had a chance of attacking.'

'The trouble is,' said Myriam, 'he seeks out the most defenceless of us, and that means the ewes. He's not going to choose to tussle with a full-grown ram.'

'Very well,' agreed Francis. 'And that brings me to the crux of the plan.' He looked at each of them, blinking his green eyes in a rather hypnotic way. Carl shifted his trotters uncomfortably.

'We need a lure,' the tabby cat whispered.

'A lure?' asked Myriam.

Carl grunted, 'It's the only way.'

'Naturally,' purred Francis, 'one of your females must

be stationed in an easy spot for the Rottweiler to pounce. In the meantime you two rams, and the pig, wait close by. Then, as the dog attacks, you rush out at it and – phfft! – end of menace.'

'No doubt there will be plenty of volunteers among the ewes to be the required sacrifice,' remarked Reuben.

'You'll have to sort that out for yourselves,' said Francis. 'One sheep dies – the rest are saved. It makes sense to me.'

'You're not a sheep,' Reuben said softly. He was beginning to dislike the arrogant attitude of this small beast who spoke to them from the vantage point of a pine branch.

'If you have any better ideas . . . .' the cat miaowed lazily, leaving the rest unsaid.

'It might be possible, Reuben,' Jacob bleated, 'to ensure the ewe doesn't die, and the basis of the cat's plan is a good one, I think.'

'What part does friend Francis intend to play whilst we're all risking ourselves?' Reuben wanted to know.

'The plan is my part in the scene,' Francis answered promptly. He stood up and stretched, raking the branch with his claws with an air of conscious superiority that really irritated the younger ram; he turned on his heel and went back to the flock. The other sheep crowded round and wanted to know what the cat's idea had been, but Reuben was unable to tell them.

Francis was now interesting himself in the possibility of catching a bird which was hopping about amongst the higher branches of the tree, so Jacob and Myriam left him to his own devices. Carl was rooting around on the ground.

'I think I have the answer to our problem,' Myriam confided to Jacob quietly.

Jacob looked at her with interest, 'I can read your

thoughts,' he said, 'because I'm sure I'm thinking the same thing.'

'Well?'

'You're thinking of using Bell as the decoy, aren't you, to punish her for plotting against you?'

Myriam was aghast. 'No, no,' she said in a pained voice, 'when have I ever been so vindictive?'

'Well, you haven't,' he admitted, 'but I would like Bell to be the choice.'

'Oh, we couldn't,' declared Myriam. 'How could we persuade her to sacrifice herself, and anyway, why should she?'

'I can think of one very strong reason. But, Myriam, we wouldn't tell her she was acting as bait; and she needn't die, we'll be there to save her.'

'No, I don't like it. But listen, I've a better idea: I myself will be the lure.'

'Never!' cried Jacob at once. 'You're not risking—'

'Jacob, let me finish,' interrupted Myriam. 'Don't you see – I'm the only animal for the job. Roger knows me of old and he's bound to hesitate when he sees it's old Myriam standing alone; that's the time to catch him.'

Jacob looked very unhappy, 'Oh Myriam,' he said, 'why are you always putting yourself in danger?'

'I don't believe I would be in danger,' she answered confidently. 'It really is the best way, perhaps the only way, to catch Roger off guard.'

'Well, I don't know,' Jacob said. 'Supposing it all went wrong? How could I live with myself?'

'Trust me,' said Myriam. 'I'm sure it's our answer. Yes, it's a risk, but a slender one; and the whole flock will then be safe. Please, let me try.'

Jacob could not resist her plea; her gentle, beseeching brown eyes, but he resolved to himself that Myriam should not lose her life through any failing on his part.

He meant to be hovering very close indeed when the Rottweiler made its appearance.

The rest of the flock were astounded when Jacob announced the plan, finding Myriam's courage almost impossible to comprehend. Reuben and Frolic raised objections at once, but she calmly overruled them; and Bell, who had bitterly regretted her plot against Myriam ever since she had perpetrated it, felt foolish and humble. She was sure the other sheep were casting reproving glances in her direction and so she kept her eyes fixed firmly on the ground. Bridget, needless to say, did not fail to notice and enjoy Bell's discomfort.

'Well, Jacob,' bleated Barley, 'here's a way for the great, wise ram to treat his favourite.' Since the unusual sensations aroused by the tupping season had well and truly subsided, she was ready to resume her role as Jacob's main critic. She almost felt it was expected of her.

Jacob was ready with a reply. 'Of course, Barley, if you're ready to volunteer in Myriam's place, I'm sure there would be no objection!'

Barley took the retort in good part. 'I don't think the flock would let me,' she murmured.

Since her continual carping often irritated the other sheep, this reply caused a ripple of amusement throughout the flock. 'Barley likes to keep us all entertained,' Frolic muttered good-humouredly.

Dancer spoke up. 'How do any of us know when the dog will be back?'

Jacob answered, 'It knows where we are, you see. It will never be far away. But we can't remain in this vicinity; we need to find a spot where there is some sort of protection. Reuben and I have to be able to hide ourselves somewhere for the plot to work.'

'Carl knows the forest best,' said Reuben. 'He's been

around a long while – let's consult him.'

They fetched the pig, who was very glad to be involved. 'I know just the place,' he told them. 'There's a gap in the trees and undergrowth used to be thick there. It will have died back by now, but might still serve our purpose.'

'Lead on, Carl,' said Jacob.

He took them into the farthest depths of the forest while Francis watched their retreat with boredom. He had caught a bird and was finding the best bits to eat.

The thick pine and fir trees seemed to cluster around the animals, shading them in darkness where the bleak light almost failed to penetrate. Only a scattering of snow underfoot lit their way, but after a while they saw the opening ahead. Carl waited at the edge of the trees, shivering as he looked at the open ground where the snow fell. There were thick clumps of dead brown bracken, loaded with white, and the ferns were a good metre in height.

'You'd be perfectly hidden in there,' the pig remarked. 'Your white coats would be almost indistinguishable.'

'Perfect,' agreed Jacob.

'I'll leave you then,' Carl said. 'My teeth are beginning to chatter. But I won't be far distant and if you need my help, I'll be pleased to give it.'

'Thank you,' said Jacob. 'Your bulk is impressive, Carl, but you would really need a pair of horns to do any real harm.'

'I can bite,' Carl retorted. 'Anyway, I really must go. The sight of all that snow makes my bones ache; it won't be long before the forest itself is submerged.'

There was not much for the sheep to do now but wait. As it grew dark the wind dropped and the snowflakes diminished to a trickle.

'I'll take my place here,' said Myriam, going right into the clearing. 'I can pretend to be grazing. Now is the time when Roger's likely to be on the prowl.'

Jacob pushed the flock well back under the trees and he and Reuben got in amongst the snow-covered bracken, one to the left of Myriam and one to the right. The sheep were as quiet as the grave; only Myriam made any noise as she scraped at the snow and bent to look for the herbage underneath. The minutes crept by and nothing broke the silence: there was no birdsong, there were no night cries. The minutes became an hour and Jacob and Reuben shifted their positions, straining to catch the slightest sound. It was now quite dark. Another half hour passed, and the moon broke through the cloud covering briefly, then vanished again. Time went on – Myriam continued her tasks of scraping the snow and nibbling. Then they heard it . . . .

To any creature who had not become so accustomed to the different noises of the wind as the sheep had, the faint sigh they now heard would have been unremarkable. But it was a different sound from any breeze or puff of wind they had heard before, and both Myriam and the two rams in their hiding place recognized it: the regular pant of a dog. Jacob and Reuben tensed. Myriam looked up momentarily, tossed her head, and bent again to the ground; but out of the corner of her eye she had seen him, slinking along, almost on his belly, under cover of the trees along the farther edge of the clearing. She knew it was Roger.

The Rottweiler saw the solitary ewe and crept closer. He knew he had to cross the clearing to get to her and he almost whined in his excitement. For a long time he hovered under the trees, meaning to run across the open ground as soon as his quarry should turn her back. His blood pounded in his veins and the urge to kill was so strong that his eyes seemed to glaze under the influence of its strange power. His whole body throbbed and his tongue lolled from his open jaws. He saw the ewe slowly turn, intent on her search for titbits under the snow. Roger started across the snowy ground, his pads sinking almost silently into the soft white mass. But there was just sufficient sound as he moved for Myriam to know he was coming. Then the dog gathered speed, building up for its spring, and as he reached a point about halfway across the clearing, Myriam swung round to face him. Roger recognized her immediately. He was going too fast to pull up, but he checked his speed instinctively, and slowed down about two metres from her. He looked unsure, but his feet kept moving and his jaws remained open. Myriam bleated sharply and Jacob and Reuben shot from their screens of ferns, heads lowered, and galloped towards the Rottweiler. To the dog, taken completely by surprise, it was as if the vegetation had suddenly exploded at him. The next instant it was as if he had been struck by a thunderbolt; the double weight of two pairs of horns crashed into him simultaneously and the killer was flattened.

Jacob and Reuben steadied themselves and looked back to see Myriam peering at the prone body of the Rottweiler, draped lifelessly over the snow just where it had fallen. The two rams returned slowly.

'Is he dead?' Reuben asked.

'I can't tell,' Myriam answered.

They all stared at the sheep killer, its limbs splayed unnaturally, its mouth agape and the hair all around the broad square muzzle matted with the dried blood of its last feasting. Its eyes were dull and unmoving.

'Roger will kill no more sheep,' Jacob pronounced solemnly.

As they continued to look, the rest of the flock came hesitatingly out from the trees, Asher in the forefront. 'I'm glad it's over,' he said to Reuben. 'But I was ready to help if necessary. I waited just inside the forest; I thought you might want me.'

'Luckily not,' Reuben answered. 'But thanks,' he added kindly.

The sheep jostled each other – they all wanted to see the beast that had preyed on them. They started to praise Jacob and Reuben as their heroes, their saviours.

'No, make no mistake,' Jacob told them, 'Myriam is the heroine of this episode. You owe your lives to her more than to any other animal.'

Myriam answered modestly, 'I think we ought not to forget that we owe something to our new acquaintance the cat.'

# —13—

# 'The Noise from the Sky'

With the threat of the killer dog removed, the flock roamed through the forest with lighter hearts, their difficulties now centred on the search for food. Snow continued to fall periodically and temperatures stayed low. The forest floor was soon spread with white, and the depth of the snow under the trees gradually increased. Carl did what he could to help the foraging but he was unable to do much. The unrelenting cold was beginning to tell on him; he suffered more and more as time went on and, with the shortage of food, lost weight rapidly. All the acorns and beech mast from the few deciduous trees had soon been snapped up by the pig or buried by squirrels. Mosses and lichen and a mouthful here and there of bulbs were all any of them could hope for now. Carl started to eat twigs and bark.

Francis was very rarely seen but when the sheep did catch a glimpse of him they could tell that life was proving difficult for him too. His ribs protruded through his fur and his green eyes had always the gleam of unsatisfied hunger in them.

At night Carl tried to nestle himself amongst the sheep when he slept, hoping to attract some extra warmth to himself from their woolly bodies. But he found they were generally very restless and he would often wake, his body almost freezing, to find he was alone. The contrast of the cold with the previous warmth was almost too severe for him to bear and he came to believe that it was only a matter of time before he would die in the forest. His one desire was that humans would appear again; but they made no further attempts to retrieve the sheep.

One day another refugee from the inhospitable moors came into the forest. It was the donkey, encountered by the flock many weeks earlier and now seeking shelter. They had seen the animal before in the company of a horse but now the donkey was alone. It was not surprised to see the sheep there, and it seemed to know Carl. 'Well, I wondered what had happened to you,' the donkey said by way of a greeting. 'I thought you had perished long ago.'

'Not quite yet,' Carl grunted, 'but this cold will be the end of me. Look at me, I'm just a shadow of my former self.'

'At least there's some protection under these trees,' said the donkey. 'I felt I could no longer face another day out there on the moors.'

'You haven't done yourself such a good turn coming in here,' Carl remarked pessimistically. 'There's no food to be had – and what happened to your pal Captain?'

'He's more at home with the wild ponies than with me; they have much more in common, and they show him how to feed in the snow and so on. But I fear for him; he hasn't their resilience.'

'We're all in the same dilemma, we animals used to human care,' Carl observed. 'Tell me, Jenny, have you seen any men on the moors?'

'No,' she brayed. 'Not one – they've more sense. But they've started to drop food for the ponies, so Captain shares the harvest.'

'Drop food?'

'Yes; batches of hay, from overhead. It comes down

very suddenly from the sky and the ponies never know exactly where it will fall. Of course, they're very glad of it.'

Carl looked pensive. 'I think our woolly friends might be interested in this,' he said. 'They're having a lean time of it.'

'Don't excite them too much,' Jenny cautioned the pig. 'The ponies make short work of the hay and they won't be very happy to share it with sheep. There isn't very much available.'

'I'll mention it anyhow,' said the pig. 'I've grown quite fond of some of them.'

Jacob's ears pricked up at once when he heard the news. The flock had taken to eating all sorts of unusual items and he was afraid of sickness. 'I wonder how we could find these food sources,' he mused.

'Come and talk to the donkey,' said Carl. 'She knows all about it.'

Jenny told them they would know when the hay was coming because they would hear a noise from the sky.

'I know what you mean,' said Jacob. 'We're quite familiar with the noise from those human homes that fly.'

'That's it,' Jenny said. 'But you'll have to be out on the moorland; you'll never hear it from the forest. The ponies roam widely and the hay always comes down in different places.'

'I'll see what the others think,' Jacob said. 'We certainly need better food.'

'Don't forget the ponies,' Jenny warned. 'They're wild and there might be trouble.'

Carl had been doing some thinking too. 'Let me know what you decide,' he said to Jacob. 'If you venture out I'll come with you. I might be spotted by these humans and then, who knows, I might be saved.'

'I understand you, Carl,' said Jacob. 'You can rely on me.'

The flock proved to be divided in its opinion about the hay. Some of the sheep longed so much for proper fodder they were prepared to take any chance to get it; others thought to take to the moors again would be futile and dangerous. Amongst these was Reuben.

'Too much of a risk,' he said, 'to expose ourselves to the worst conditions for a wisp or two of dry grass. It's more than likely the ponies would corner the supply, and we'd be no competition for them.'

Bridget, who had lost much of her fat, like many of the other ewes, argued that she dreamed all the time of the taste of grass, and that she for one would be prepared to withstand any rigours to taste it once more.

'You're ignoring the really important point,' Reuben remarked.

Jacob knew what was in his mind.

'There's nothing more important than eating properly,' Bridget declared. 'Most of the ewes are carrying lambs, and mosses and bits of wood will hardly sustain them.'

'And what if we're seen by our human benefactors?' Reuben demanded. 'We could find ourselves locked up in one of their great barns before we'd chewed so much as a stalk!'

'Don't exaggerate, Reuben,' said his sister Frolic, who was also pregnant. 'In any case, it might be the best outcome for us females; we shall need a bit of comfort.'

'I don't propose to move from this forest,' returned Reuben stubbornly. 'And I don't want Snow and my other followers to leave either.'

'They have no say in the matter of their diet, I suppose?' snapped Frolic. 'I hope Jess doesn't feel like that.'

'Of course I don't,' Jess reassured her at once. 'You know best about that.'

Jacob intervened hastily. He could see that the flock was in danger of being split up again. 'Let's wait awhile,' he advised, 'at least until we're sure the hay is still being brought. Otherwise we could lose our shelter for nothing.'

There were some mumblings and murmurings but no animal voiced any argument against this.

Conditions remained the same, and soon the New Year had begun. Carl had been very disappointed to see the sheep remain in the forest and was close to despair about his own fate; he had not the will to leave the forest on his own and now he spent more and more time in his litter. The litter increased constantly in size as Carl gathered more brushwood, pine needles, dead leaves and bracken, in a constant battle to combat the ever-present cold. He used his snout to push it into piles around him but, since he still suffered as much as ever, all his attempts to gain some warmth were in vain.

One day he was trying hard to doze in his comfortless bed when Francis walked by. Carl saw him undulating past with his easy, effortless grace and noticed the cat's exceptionally spare frame. 'We're all going to die in here before much longer,' the pig grunted.

The cat stopped with one front paw uplifted and turned his beautiful green eyes on the mound of debris Carl had collected together. 'In there?' he drawled. 'But why should any other creature enter your strange construction?'

'No, I don't mean in here, in my litter,' Carl answered, 'and I'm sure you didn't think I did. I was referring to the forest.'

Francis came closer and looked in. 'Oh, I don't think any of us need die,' he said coolly, 'now the killer is no longer around to cause us problems.'

'I'm glad you're so confident,' muttered the pig. 'You don't look in the full bloom of health to me.'

'I get by,' Francis replied. 'Things will improve.'

'Don't you ever long for the warmth of a sty and some clean straw?'

'Not really – as a farm cat I wasn't mollycoddled, and I never did live in a sty. But I do take your point. There were times when I could scorch my fur in front of a great fire and never want to move again.'

'Oh warmth! Will this cold never end?'

'Yes, it will end. It always does. The thaw will come and soon we'll hardly remember what it was like.'

'I shall,' Carl retorted. 'I'll never forget this as long as I live – and that won't be very long.'

'Don't be so pessimistic, my friend,' Francis told him. 'Try and be more cheerful.' The cat went on his way.

'It's all right for him,' Carl said to himself. 'It can't take much to keep a little scrap like him warm.'

About a week after this, Jenny the donkey came looking for Carl. She had left the confines of the forest briefly to dig under the snow for heather shoots and she told the pig that she had heard the noise from the sky again.

'Did you see anything?' Carl questioned her eagerly.

'No,' she answered. 'The noise was quite faint. There are no ponies at all in this quarter.'

'Don't tell the sheep that or they'll never leave here,' Carl said miserably. He was unaware that a new factor had emerged to influence the flock's movement. Several of the sheep were sick.

Despite Jacob's constant warnings, it had been almost inevitable that there would be sickness, given the shortage of proper fodder in the forest. There was no herbage; no heather to nibble. The sheep had come to rely more and more on twigs and tree bark with growths of lichen.

Resinous and oily, small quantities might have been taken without mishap, but over a long period of time they proved poisonous. The older ewes succumbed first – one of them was Martha; she lost all appetite, vomited and became very weak. Then three or four others began to show the same symptoms.

'Winter or no winter,' Myriam said to Jacob, 'we've got to move from here. The flock must have proper food.'

'I know,' he answered. 'I've decided what to do. I shall go to search for the hay now, while the weather is clear. You and Reuben must keep the flock in order and try to see they only eat what is safe. I'll look for the ponies.'

Jacob set off. He spoke first to Jenny, wondering if she had any idea which direction he should take.

'I'll go with you part of the way,' she volunteered.

The day was crisp, cold and bright. The snow that had fallen at intervals now for weeks reflected the sun's rays and the whole countryside glistened like one vast jewel. Jacob's spirits revived as he left the trees behind; he felt freer and more lively than for a long time. The gloom and closeness of the forest seemed to have hung over him like an extra fleece.

Jenny led the way. She moved easily over the snow which, since the end of the gales, was more evenly spread. Jacob followed behind her without speaking, pondering the flock's survival. After a while he was startled from his thoughts by the donkey opening her mouth wide and braying suddenly and very loudly. She had spied her old companion Captain ahead of them and called a greeting. The horse answered, giving a whinny of pleasure. Jacob could see a few ponies nearby and Captain towered over them. Jenny ran on ahead.

Jacob soon spotted that there was no hay. But the ponies could see he was searching the snow.

'It's all gone,' one of them commented drily. 'It doesn't last long, you know.'

'I'm sorry,' said Jacob, embarrassed at his actions being interpreted so easily. 'The sheep are in a bit of a plight. I might as well be honest with you, they're becoming ill through eating the forest debris.'

Jenny and Captain had finished exchanging their greetings, and were listening. The horse said, 'We were hoping for more to be brought. We expected it yesterday – and today. We've been wandering around in case it came down somewhere else.'

'Have you heard the noise from the sky?' Jenny asked him promptly.

'Not for some days,' Captain admitted. 'But even when we do hear it, we sometimes get no food. There are other ponies, you see, scattered about.'

'Wherever you search,' the pony said to Jacob, 'there's hardly likely to be enough for a flock of sheep as well as ourselves.'

Jacob felt awkward. He wondered if his presence was resented, then a thought struck him. 'Would more hay be brought if more animals were seen on the moors?' he asked.

'That's a clever notion,' Captain remarked with surprise. 'I always thought sheep were rather stupid creatures.'

'Not all of us,' Jacob answered, wryly. 'What do you think?'

'It might work,' the pony said. 'And it might not. You and Captain and Jenny there must know more about human behaviour than we do.'

'I certainly think there's a good chance of it,' the horse remarked.

'Poor Carl might get his share then as well as his greatest wish,' said Jenny.

'Yes, it's not the hay he's interested in,' Jacob added.

'Who's Carl?' asked the pony.

'A pig who lost his home just like us,' Jenny explained.

'A pig? Well, we shall have a real farmyard collection here, shan't we?' The pony sounded disgruntled. The other ponies muttered between themselves, thinking of the consequences to their stomachs if there should be no increase in the provision of hay.

'We don't want to be thought greedy, do we?' Captain urged them. 'It seems the sheep are really suffering.'

'We didn't ask all of you to come up here in the first place,' one of the other ponies pointed out testily. 'We constitute the moorland grazing population: the hay is meant for us.'

'We didn't ask for the flood,' Jacob replied. 'We have a right to survive too, you know.'

There was silence while the ponies weighed Jacob's words. Most of them looked sullen; it was as if they recognized the sheep's rights but resented them. At length one of them spoke.

'All right,' he said. 'We'll take a chance. You bring your flock out here at your own risk and if it results in more food we'll share it out with you.' He looked at his companions for their agreement, and none of them argued. 'But,' the pony went on, 'you must abide by our terms; so that if there is no extra fodder you go without. Is that understood?'

Jacob was in no position to argue. He agreed readily and thanked the ponies. 'I'll inform the others,' he said.

Jenny remained behind. It seemed she did not want to be parted again from Captain, and Jacob wondered if there was more than just friendship between them. He returned to the forest and explained the plan.

'I'll have no part of it,' Reuben declared at once. 'It's inviting capture.'

'It's inviting death to stay in here – you'll starve,' Bridget said sharply.

'How are the sick ones?' Jacob interrupted, turning to Myriam.

'About the same – no improvement,' she answered.

'You see, Reuben,' Jacob reasoned, 'that's your real danger. There's nothing good left to eat here. Please, consider your ewes, don't sacrifice them. We evaded the humans before and we can do it again.'

Reuben wavered. He did not care to be seen to succumb to Jacob's persuasin, though, believing that it would be seen as a sign of weakness in himself by Snow and his other females. So he said, 'You go with those who wish to follow you, Jacob; I won't stand in any animal's way.' But he added subtly, 'I hope my little flock will remain loyal to me.'

'Come, then,' said Jacob. 'The weather's clear and there's no time to be lost. We might all have full stomachs again by the end of the day.'

The sheep gathered eagerly but, just as they were about to set off, Francis could be seen picking his way over the snow towards them. Jacob lingered a little since the cat appeared to have something to tell them.

'There's an interesting development,' Francis announced.

'Development? What do you mean?' the sheep bleated all at once.

'The Rottweiler's disappeared,' the cat said.

There was a stunned silence. It was Jacob who broke it, 'I think you mean the carcass of the Rottweiler, for that was all that was left of it.' His voice sounded hollow.

'Carcass?' queried Francis. 'What sort of creature

could have carried off such a large body?'

None of the sheep had the answer to that, but they all knew what the cat's words meant. Was the Rottweiler dead after all?

# —14—

# 'Make Yourselves Seen'

Jacob hastily brought the animals' minds back to the immediate topic of food and, without further talk, he led the sheep out from the trees into the snowy landscape. Reuben and about half a dozen ewes watched the flock depart; some of Reuben's own females had joined the throng. The sick animals too, had to stay behind. Francis climbed a tree; he had decided to spend most of his time in the branches, until the truth about the dog's disappearance was known.

Jacob's brain was in a whirl. How could the Rottweiler have lain there in extreme cold for days, to all appearances lifeless, and yet have recovered? Then he realized that none of the sheep had returned to the scene of the ambush since his and Reuben's attack, so the dog might have limped away on regaining its strength, after a matter of hours. Or had something else, human or beast, removed it? The uncertainty was horrible and Jacob knew that it would hang like a dark shadow over all of them. How or when this shadow could be dispelled he did not dare to contemplate.

The group of wild ponies had wandered on, Jenny and Captain with them. When the flock appeared, the ponies looked rather sour at their numbers, but they voiced no complaint. The sheep began to chew at the heather exposed by the ponies' scraping and the plant tasted

sweet after their strange diet. Time passed and there was
no sound heralding the approach of an aircraft. It grew
dark. The ponies had been forgotten, and cold gripped
each and every animal.

'I suppose there will be more hay?' Jenny muttered.

'Who knows? It might stop as suddenly as it started,'
answered a pony fatalistically. 'But we'll get through
somehow – we always do.'

The sheep took little comfort from these words. They
were not quite so hardy and the pregnant ewes were
thinking constantly of their unborn lambs. A biting wind
sprang up, driving over the moors with a cruel strength.
Jacob knew that snow was coming; the air itself was like
ice. He decided to return to shelter, the flock following
him willingly. Jenny and the horse joined them all under
the pine trees.

Before they had reached the forest the snow came
whirling across from the east with such severity that it was
as if a screen had been dropped suddenly in front of
them, cutting them off from the rest of the world. They
could see nothing; hear nothing. They plodded on
without altering direction, the only protection for any of
them coming from the animal immediately in front. For
the donkey and the horse there was none at all.

Jacob, at the head of the flock, battled blindly onwards
with only instinct to guide him. Because of the conditions, he could not tell if any of the sheep had got into
trouble and dropped behind. One had, Bell, in her cus-
tomary position at the very rear of the column.

For a long time, since the perpetration of her trick on
Myriam, she had felt an outcast in the flock. She followed
the others at a distance and very soon the heavy swirl of
flakes hid not only the sheep, but also the tall figure of
Captain from her sight. She began to wander from the
correct course and, stumbling and sinking into the new

soft snow, she was soon lost in the whiteness. The wind formed drifts, and Bell plunged into the middle of one without a warning, unable to get herself out again. After floundering helplessly for a while and sinking further and further, she became very tired and seemed to accept her end.

It's the best thing for me, she thought. I deserve it. One is always punished for one's wrongs in the end. The snow drove down relentlessly and eventually buried her.

Some time later in the forest, where the flock huddled together, trying to find warmth in their companions' closeness, Bridget noticed Bell's absence. But she said nothing; she thought of Bell as her enemy and she was glad she was gone.

Reuben told Jacob that two of the sick sheep had died, and that it looked likely that the rest would not last very much longer. Jacob was at his wits' end: the sheep could not stay in the forest because of the danger of sickness, and outside, the weather might claim them. And there was the renewed threat of the Rottweiler prowling on the loose. Jacob had secretly accepted that the dog was still alive and, worse still, out for revenge. He felt crushed under the burden of leadership. How could he save the flock?

'I fear for us, Myriam,' he groaned to the faithful ewe. 'We're in a trap; death threatens us from all sides.'

She was unable to bring him comfort. She felt his words to be true and she was very frightened.

Carl, a shadow of his former self, came slowly from his bed to discover what success the sheep had found. But when he saw the flock, huddled and shivering in their misery, he did not dare ask. He wormed his way into the depth of the throng, ignoring the snowy fleeces, grateful even for the illusion of extra warmth. This time none of the animals stirred and Carl grunted his gratitude.

Jenny and Captain stood uncertainly. The donkey's patience was limitless, but the long-legged, gaunt horse no longer had any confidence in his own survival now that the supplies of hay seemed to have been curtailed.

Francis watched them all from his pine branch and could not help but sympathize with them. He knew nothing of the hoped-for hay but he knew perfectly well they were all at the end of their tethers. From his lofty position he was aware of much that went on in that part of the forest: he could see squirrels jumping through the branches, birds flying from tree to tree in their day-long quest for food; hear the sounds of owls or other night hunters from time to time. And, at dusk, a sound which nearly made his blood run cold – the howl of a dog. He suspected the worst, but nothing on earth would have made him leave the tree to warn the flock. He calculated they would all discover the source of the sound before very much longer.

Towards morning the blizzard blew itself out and the animals' hopes lifted a fraction with the return of the daylight. Jenny walked slowly to the edge of the trees and looked out disconsolately, she could not even recognize the spot where the ponies had stood in the wilderness of white. The whole landscape was as empty of life as a mountain top. Then she heard it – the drone of an aeroplane.

Instantly she brayed a signal to the others. Captain galloped forward; he had heard the noise too. 'Come on!' he whinnied in his excitement. 'Make yourselves seen!'

The sheep leapt to life, barging and colliding with one another in their haste to be the first into the open. Carl was buffeted on all sides. He had lain down amongst all the feet and drifted off to sleep in his new-found luxury. A rush of icy air roused him to wakefulness and he saw the sheep running. He lumbered after them, eager not to be overlooked if humans were around. In the end only Reuben remained under the canopy of branches; even his ewes had succumbed and become part of the general stampede for food.

The aircraft was approaching, a glistening speck in the brilliant blue sky. The sheep surged through the thick blanket of snow, leaping and heaving themselves through the mass, moving forward with determination.

'The noise from the sky, the noise from the sky,' Jenny was almost singing in her unmusical voice to Captain, whose hooves kicked up a constant spray of snow and ice.

It was no time at all before the machine was directly overhead and square bales of hay were dropped noiselessly through the stinging cold of the air. They landed with muffled thuds to the right and left of the animals; before them and behind them.

Ponies came charging into view as if from nowhere and, in a moment or two, the bales were being torn apart by their strong teeth. The aircraft vanished, but not before its occupants had noticed the sheep. There was plenty of hay for the ponies but many of the sheep went without, Jacob included. He tried to see that the pregnant ewes got their feed first and it was whilst he was overseeing this that he missed Bell for the first time.

The unfed sheep were bickering over the remnants of stalks scattering the snow and Jacob and the young rams chewed heathertips from a patch which was not entirely covered. The unsatisfied sheep protested to Jacob about their hunger.

'You'll be first next time,' he told them.

'When will that be?' they wanted to know, ignoring the fact that he, too, was hungry.

'Soon,' he promised them. 'We must have been noticed.'

Carl was excited, 'Do you really think so, Jacob?'

'I'm sure of it,' the ram answered kindly, touched by his eagerness. 'Your sufferings will soon be over.'

'One way or another they surely will be,' Carl remarked.

Two of the ponies wandered over. 'Now we shall all see if your plan works, ram,' one of them said.

'But remember our terms,' the other pony cautioned.

'I will. But it's scarcely necessary,' Jacob answered. 'We sheep are no match for you. You're faster, stronger and fitter than any of us.'

The sheep wandered around whilst the day remained clear, not knowing exactly what they should do next. There were no further signs of human presence either above or on Leckmoor, and when the sky clouded over again, Jacob sensed bad weather was approaching. He led the retreat to the forest, and this time the flock was under the trees before the first flakes fell.

Reuben watched their return moodily. He felt he had missed out on something, yet he was offended by his females' lack of loyalty, particularly Snow, his favourite.

'I wasn't being disloyal,' she remarked. 'You're too stubborn, Reuben, with your ideas. I've eaten some real fodder at last, which can only be good for my lamb; if I'd stayed here with you I'd still be famished.'

The young ram could see that there was sense in this, but he continued to feel slighted. He noticed Jacob was looking around expectantly. 'Who are you searching for, Jacob?' he asked.

'Bell. Isn't she here?'

'No – only obstinate Reuben and the sick sheep stayed behind,' Bridget muttered.

'But where is she then?'

'Under the snow, I hope,' Bridget whispered wickedly, but not loud enough to be heard.

'I think we must have left her behind somewhere,' Myriam remarked.

'Who saw her last?' Jacob asked quickly.

There were no replies and it became clear that Bell had been missing for quite some time.

'The blizzard!' Becky exclaimed. 'She was behind me then, I'm sure. But after that, I don't know . . . .'

'Poor Bell!' bleated Frolic.

'She can't have gone far astray,' said Myriam. 'I wonder why she hasn't come back to us?' She looked at Jacob, read what was in his eyes, and looked away again hastily. The dog!

Jacob was genuinely sorry that he had not taken more care to see that all the animals had come in from the storm the previous day. He forgot his feelings about Bell – he would not have had this happen for the world.

'She won't come back now, I'm afraid,' chanted Barley. 'Another sheep lost.' She did not say any more but Jacob knew full well what she was suggesting.

'It's up to all of us to look out for one another,' Jess said. 'Those at the front can't see what's happening at the back – especially in a blizzard.'

The snowflakes were filtering down now through the branches at a steady pace and Jacob suddenly felt very forlorn. 'I wish I could see just a little way into the future,' he said quietly.

Myriam's ears pricked up; she had never heard such a plaintive note in Jacob's voice before. He was always so calm and strong, he was their only hope. They all depended on him and if he should lose heart now . . . .

'Jacob,' she said, trying to put a soothing, calming note into her tired old voice. 'Come with me a short way. I think we should talk together.'

Jacob went willingly. Myriam was the only animal who might be able to provide him with some comfort.

As soon as the two sheep were at a slight distance from the flock, Myriam urged Jacob not to give up hope. 'This can't go on for ever,' she said. 'We can still make it. Think, if the hay is provided again tomorrow, we'll see things in a different way. We mustn't give up. You mustn't. Only you can see us through.'

'Oh, Myriam,' said Jacob, his voice weary. 'I have my limits. I can do nothing about Roger, and I know he's prowling around. We were foolish, we could at least have ended that threat.'

'You didn't know,' she answered hurriedly. 'None of us did. We all assumed that—'

'Yes,' he broke in. 'How stupid of us – to assume a dog like that could be disposed of by sheep!'

'He very nearly was and that last encounter may have changed his mind about us.'

'Oh no!' Jacob responded. 'He's cunning and he'll be waiting his chance. He's had Bell, I'm certain, and he'll be skulking in the forest, waiting to pick off the next one.'

'Has he the strength now?' Myriam persisted. 'I think he must be very much weakened after the blow you and Reuben dealt him. And we won't give him the opportunity to attack again. He can't separate the flock, and there will be no sheep standing around on their own inviting him to attack like I did.'

'Where are the sick ones?' Jacob asked suddenly. 'There's no guard for them.'

'We left them by Carl's litter,' said Myriam, 'and Reuben has been around. But the poor creatures are more likely to survive the Rottweiler's sly ways than their own sufferings.'

'I might be overestimating the dog's strength,' Jacob said on reflection. 'And, Myriam, I'll do my best for all of us.'

'I know, and you know I'll be behind you.'

'Oh, if it weren't for you . . . .' Jacob began. He did not need to finish.

That night the flock kept close together, near to Carl's litter. It was bitterly cold. Jacob and Myriam lay next to the pig, one on either side; they wanted no more deaths. Jenny and Captain stood under the pines and shivered through the dark hours. Out in the snow, Bell spent her second night buried. The snow shielded her a little from the cruel temperatures, but she found nothing but dry lichens to eat where she scraped underfoot. She made no effort to free herself.

By the morning the three remaining sick animals in the flock had died. Jacob was philosophical about their loss, at least they were safe from Roger. But from now on he was determined that every animal in the Sweetriver flock would have as good a chance of survival as he could provide. He was the oldest of them, and if anyone had to die, it should be him. But not yet.

He had high hopes of eating hay that day, and this would enable the sheep to renew their strength and would mean the lambs would be born healthy in the spring, so that the flock's losses could be replenished. But how distant the spring seemed. Human help would make all the difference now.

It was still snowing. The flakes fell almost vertically in the absence of any wind and, when the snow finally stopped around noon, Jacob was sure the air felt warmer. Jenny and Captain had already left the forest to be ready for the noise from the sky – now it was time the sheep left too.

'Follow me, all of you,' Jacob said. 'I'm confident we shall all be feeding soon.'

Reuben watched the animals pass him, one by one, the pig included. Would none of them stay with him? He looked at Snow, but she kept her eyes on the sheep in front of her, and only Asher turned to look at his old companion with something of regret.

'Asher?' Reuben muttered, catching his eye. It was an unconscious appeal but Asher wanted badly to eat and passed by. He only pleaded, 'Join us, Reuben! There will be food.'

Reuben was adamant. If the flock had been seen, the humans might come at any time – let them all be taken, he was safe from discovery.

The flock halted behind Jacob at the point where they had gathered the previous day.

'We've heard nothing yet,' the donkey told them.

'Where do the ponies go?' asked Becky. 'They don't seem to be around.'

'Oh, they'll come soon enough, never fear,' said Captain. 'Just as soon as they catch the first faint whiff of hay.'

Carl was sniffing the air and grunting to himself. 'It's warmer, it's warmer – I'm certain of it,' he said delightedly.

'I thought so too,' Jacob agreed. 'But don't get too excited, Carl, it's early days yet.'

The animals roamed about expectantly. Jacob mused on the possibility of the food being dropped elsewhere, and he constantly scanned the horizon all around for any sign of ponies. At last the familiar droning hum they were all impatient for was heard. The sheep bleated happily to each other. Captain whinnied and Jenny brayed. The aircraft's arrival was celebrated enthusiastically and then, just as before, ponies were seen dotting the landscape as they ran over the snow.

The amount of hay was more plentiful this time.

'Get your heads down, everyone,' Captain quipped, 'the ponies are coming.'

But it did not matter, every animal found sufficient food. Even Carl ate, although hay was something quite new to him. The wild ponies who knew Jacob had to acknowledge that his plan had worked.

'Don't expect much more of this sky fodder, though,' one of them cautioned him. 'There's a thaw coming.'

Jacob looked at him quickly. 'How can you tell?'

'We've lived around here in all sorts of weather for long enough to know such things,' was the reply.

Jacob pondered. A thaw would mean the flock could find its own food again. It would also mean that there was a good chance that men would come to round up the sheep and other strays like Carl, too. It would be good news for the pig, but would it be good for the flock? Jacob realized he did not know any longer.

For some time Reuben stood unmoving in the forest after the others had left. He felt quite alone and began to think he had been behaving rather stupidly. But Reuben was not quite alone.

The cat had, for once, eaten well. More by luck than through any particular skill, he had caught a squirrel who had chosen to run along the branch on which he was crouching. Francis found it a very satisfying meal and since then, he had been cat-napping on a broader branch of the same tree. He had seen the movement of the flock, as usual; and he saw the solitary Reuben. Francis did not understand the reasons behind Reuben's solitude. He realized there was something of significance in his refusal to join the rest of the flock but he could appreciate, from his lofty haven, how vulnerable a lone sheep would be on the ground. Especially with the mystery of the Rottweiler's disappearance unsolved!

Even as the thought occurred to Francis, further away under the trees he detected a movement. There was a large, dark shape moving slowly and, it seemed, rather awkwardly amongst the pines and firs. The animal stopped suddenly and something familiar in its particular stance told Francis all he needed to know: it was Roger! Francis watched a little longer and the dog began to move again. Now Francis could see that he did indeed move with difficulty. Surely he would be seeking revenge.

Francis arched his back and hissed involuntarily. Reuben looked up but could not see the cat. Noiselessly, Francis descended the tree.

'Young ram,' he whispered urgently from the bottom. 'If you've any sense you'll leave the forest now.'

Reuben's head swung round in surprise; he was startled.

'No need to fear me,' emphasized the cat. 'There's another creature stealing through the trees you do have cause to fear, thought.'

Reuben guessed at once that Roger had finally appeared. 'Where is he?' he bleated sharply.

'Too close for comfort,' Francis whispered. 'Get going, there's no time for talk.' With a bound he leapt at the trunk of the tree and raced up it with hasty scrabbles and scratches of his claws.

Reuben started to move away, but turned once, to look back. He needed to know where exactly the dog was. He saw it at once and with alarm: Roger was much closer than he had expected. Reuben shot towards the edge of the forest and into the open moorland, then he allowed himself another glance behind. The dog had difficulty in moving quickly and had not attempted a chase. Reuben breathed more freely, he recognized that the Rottweiler was a pitiful shadow of the powerful killer it had once been. Its injuries were severe, and its locomotion jerky, more of a hobble than a walk. Anything approaching a run was out of the question, yet it was still a threat to the sheep as long as its great jaws were intact. Only by stealth and complete surprise could Roger now hope to catch his victim unawares, and Reuben knew that that was exactly the method the dog would employ.

He went on now, without any further hesitation, to rejoin the flock. He knew what he must do: firstly, he must warn Jacob and all the others that Roger had made his appearance; then lead the little group of ewes he had hoped were loyal to his leadership away from the forest for good, to another part of the moors where they would be safe from discovery by any party of humans that should come looking.

When he arrived at the place where the other sheep and the ponies, horse, donkey and pig were contentedly munching the sweet-smelling hay, Reuben's stomach took control. Without a word, he went to the nearest available supply and tore off a mouthful. The other sheep looked at him but said nothing; the business of eating was far too important to be interrupted.

It was quite a long time before Reuben's great hunger was satisfied – only his own obstinacy had enabled him to ignore its demands before. No grass he had ever eaten before in his short life, no matter how fresh and succulent, had tasted so good. In the end it was Jacob who approached Reuben.

'I'm glad you've seen sense,' he told him.

'I've seen more than that,' Reuben answered. 'Our suspicions are justified. The Rottweiler is alive – and searching.'

'Where have you seen him?' asked Jacob hurriedly in a low voice. He did not want any unnecessary alarm.

Reuben explained and described the look of the dog. At this Jacob relaxed a little. 'We may not have too much to worry about, then,' he said, 'if he's that slow. One of us can always stay awake.'

'One of us? You mean you and me?'

'No, Reuben. Asher can be involved, and Jess, and maybe Dancer and Prancer.'

'Good,' said Reuben. 'Because I don't think I can help for much longer.'

'I suppose you mean to go your own way again?'

'Yes, Jacob. You and I have different attitudes to humans.'

'You seemed to be quite appreciative just now.'

'Of course; I was starving,' Reuben said dismissively. 'But I'm taking a longer view; this hay will not be our only link with them.'

'You're right; I admit it. Now they know we are still on these moors, they won't leave us alone much longer.'

'I'll decide my fate,' Reuben declared, 'and that of my females. What will you do?'

'I shall stay to see if we're to receive more supplies,' Jacob answered. 'My chief concern is for the flock to be well fed, especially the pregnant ewes. We've had our losses and the most important thing now is for the spring to bring many healthy lambs.'

'Naturally,' agreed Reuben. 'As far as that goes, we're of one mind – but how long will you risk the flock here whilst you listen for the noise from the sky?'

'Long enough. No longer,' Jacob pronounced.

'Could be too long,' Reuben muttered. He did not know if his father had heard. Then he said, 'Jacob, I'm going to collect the ewes together and go now. I feel the worst of the weather is behind us and we'll find food. I'll see to that.'

'It's clearly no good trying to dissuade you,' Jacob remarked. 'But are you sure you know enough to get by – conditions up here are unfamiliar even to me.'

'I've learnt a lot,' said the young ram. 'And I'll learn more as I go along.'

'I understand your motives, Reuben. But I'm afraid for you.'

Reuben stood a moment longer as if his father's doubts were repeated in his own mind. But he tossed them aside with a shake of his head, and walked off purposefully to find Snow.

# —15—

# To Remain Free

Reuben, Snow, and most of the other ewes he had originally collected together made off into the bleakness of wintry Leckmoor. Reuben had failed to persuade two of his ewes to go with him. They saw a more comfortable future in store for them remaining behind with the flock, especially since there was a chance they might be rounded up and provided with shelter by the humans. Indeed, most of the pregnant ewes in the main flock had come to the conclusion that all they should be concerned about was giving birth in comfort and safety. And they were content to leave Jacob to decide what was best for them.

The beginning of the thaw was causing the snow to shrink back little by little and, as the drifts slowly melted, Bell began to struggle afresh in her snowy dungeon. She was quite weak and very stiff, but she made sufficient effort for her movements to be detected by Reuben, who happened to be leading his ewes in that direction. He saw the pile of snow being agitated by something below, and paused, fascinated by this puzzling sight. Then he heard Bell's muffled bleats.

In another moment the loose soft snow caved in and Bell's head appeared. She continued to kick and scrape but she could not manage to climb out. Reuben found it difficult to believe his eyes.

She saw him. 'Reuben!' she called faintly.

The other ewes ran over and Reuben managed to shake himself out of his astonishment. In no time, he and the ewes had butted and pushed Bell to freedom. Immediately, her legs collapsed under her and she sprawled on the surface, head first.

'She needs feeding,' said Snow.

'We must take her to the hay before it's all eaten,' said another ewe. 'Myriam will look after her.'

'No!' begged Bell weakly. 'Not Myriam. She won't want me back. This is my punishment,' she spluttered, 'I can't go back now.'

'What's she saying?' the ewes asked each other, none of them fully understanding the situation.

'She can't walk,' said Reuben. 'Not yet.'

'We can't leave her here,' said Snow. 'We must help her.'

'Of course,' he said. 'We'll fetch hay for her – all of us. Come on, there's no time to lose.'

Jacob watched their return with surprise, misled into thinking that Reuben had paid heed to his words. He was soon put right.

'I hope there's no objection,' Reuben said, 'if my ewes take a mouthful or two of hay with them to see them on their way. It all adds to the cud to chew.'

There was no dissent. Jacob was nonplussed: it did not seem to him that Reuben was making sense. What possible difference could a few extra wisps of hay make?

They were soon on their way again, and when they reached Bell they found that she had managed to get herself into a more regular position of repose. They dropped their mouthfuls by her side and she made quick work of them. She had been doing some thinking whilst she had waited for their return.

'Reuben,' she said, 'have you decided to leave the flock again?'

'Yes,' he answered promptly. 'Jacob and I don't see eye to eye on everything.' He did not go into details.

'I thought as much,' Bell went on. 'I'd like to come with you ... much better for me,' she finished, almost inaudibly. It would get her away from Bridget as well as Myriam, and she could start to breathe more freely again.

'So you shall,' said Snow kindly. 'Shan't she, Reuben?'

'Well, yes, if she wishes to,' he said uncertainly. 'But Bell, the trouble is you can't move much yet, and we can't stay here.'

'I'll be all right in a bit,' she managed to say.

'We can wait a while, I suppose,' Reuben told her. 'But we have to find some sort of shelter.'

'Where do the ponies go?' Snow asked suddenly.

'Ponies? I don't know; why?'

'We could go where they go. They must know what to do to avoid the worst weather and they didn't come into the forest.'

'No. They knew there was nothing to eat,' Reuben remarked shrewdly. He considered for a while. 'Yes, Snow. Yours is a good idea. When Bell is ready we'll follow the ponies.'

The warmer air, as well as the good fodder, helped to revive Bell quite quickly. She began to feel more hopeful about herself altogether now that she was to become part of a group of animals who seemed kindly disposed toward her.

So they set off again. Reuben, aping Jacob unconsciously, walked stiffly at the head of his females. Bell got herself into the middle of them, feeling that her days as a lone straggler were over.

They watched a group of ponies who had moved away

from where the bales of hay had been dropped. The ponies had eaten well and were going to drink from a marshy pond in a depression in the ground. The ice on the pond was melting and there was water on the surface and the ponies drank gratefully. Reuben and the others drank too, except Bell who had swallowed a lot of snow whilst she had been buried and was not thirsty.

'Where are you heading for now?' Reuben asked the ponies.

'Why are you so interested?' one of them replied.

'We thought you might lead us to some shelter,' Reuben said frankly.

'Have you abandoned the forest?'

'Yes. It's become a hostile place.'

'I see. Well, there is other cover, though not so extensive.'

'Enough to last us through the rest of the cold?'

'I can't tell you that,' the pony said at once. 'It seems there's a thaw for the present, but it could change back again just as quickly. You learn to expect anything on these moors and I've spent five seasons here. I don't know what sort of cover you're looking for?'

'Something we could hide in if necessary,' Reuben told him. 'We don't want to be rounded up.'

'Hm, I daresay a bit of dense thicket might serve. Plenty of that around – I'll show you.'

Jacob had been trying to decide what to do. He felt the flock's spell in the forest was over now and that the likelihood of human presence on the moors had to be faced. He began to question the others, ewes and rams, about their wishes. Predictably, the mothers-to-be amongst the females thought mostly of the prospect of warmth and shelter and a constant supply of nourishing fodder. The other ewes were non-committal and the rams, all of whom were so respectful toward Jacob by now, really wanted him to decide for them.

'You see,' Jacob said to all the sheep, 'we have to be quite sure if we want to return to human care or not. If any of you have a single lingering thought about enjoying again the freedom of the moors once we allowed ourselves to be rounded up and penned by Man, you should realize that that would be impossible. We should be back to our old existence, and you must be sure which you prefer in the long run. I'll give you time to think about it. Reuben and his ewes have made their minds up; they don't mean to be caught. Now we all have to make up ours.'

As he spoke to them, a realization of his true position came to Jacob for the very first time. Since the flood he had become almost a substitute figure for the sheep farmer. In his long life he had never known a period before of such freedom, such power and such importance. He had decided to lead the flock up to the moors, he had controlled their lives almost every moment since Kep had been dealt with. If they went back to the pens under the subjugation of a sheepdog, all of that would be denied to him and he would never have such a position of authority again. Despite all the fears and the concerns involved in this present existence, he knew now that he preferred it: it was life.

Jacob knew he had not many seasons left; maybe only one more. He knew now that he wanted to end it like this – free and independent, not confined and controlled. He spoke his thoughts – or some of them – to Myriam.

'Jacob,' she said, 'I'm so glad you feel as I do. It would be a betrayal to succumb now to the hand of Man, after our sufferings and our losses. Let's stay free.'

Jacob looked at the old ewe with a sort of reverence. Despite his unwaveringly deep attachment to Myriam, she had never before seemed more worthy than she did now.

'We've come this far,' he said, with all his old dignity. 'We're still a flock. We don't need the human shield.'

Some of the ewes nearest the two elders overheard these last words and caught a spark of Jacob's feelings. His nobility had returned to him; it was in his bearing, proud and majestic. They seemed to look at the ram anew.

The flicker of independence ran through the flock as they turned their heads one by one to look at Jacob. He met their glance steadily, his broad impassive head set firmly on the massive shoulders. He looked in every way a leader. Even Carl noticed this strange occurrence and he knew that the flock would go its own way.

Jacob held the flock's gaze a moment longer. Then he said simply, 'We shall stay free.'

The decision was made. None of the sheep, not even those who moments before had wished to return to human care, felt the slightest desire to disagree. Even Barley was silent. All the flock knew that they were safe under Jacob's leadership. What was best for him was best for them, too, and they were content.

Carl trotted forward. 'I sense we're about to part,' he said. 'I hope it isn't for ever.'

'Our paths are unlikely to cross again,' Jacob said honestly. 'Rescue will come for you soon. We will stay as part of the moorland population as long as we can, and see another generation of the Sweetriver flock roam this countryside.'

'I wish you luck,' said Carl.

Jacob looked at him with some regret, tinged with an unusual touch of humour. 'I wish you warmth,' he joked. But he said it with sincerity.

Jenny and Captain had already wandered away in the

company of some of the ponies. The kinder temperatures had lessened their need for the forest's protection.

Jacob led the flock away. 'We'll put the forest behind us,' he said; then in an undertone, 'Roger will find he has nothing to hunt.'

Giving themselves plenty of space, the flock skirted the forest and moved on, taking the opposite direction to that taken by Reuben. Even at that early stage of the year there was a hint that Spring was hovering, waiting for the first opportunity to blow its warm breath over Leckmoor. Jacob's heart was light and the spirits of every animal in the flock rose in sympathy. From the edge of the forest the Rottweiler watched the flock pass, light of step, their bodies swinging rhythmically; but his dull eyes sought out one animal in particular and fastened on him. In a low, drawn-out snarl he growled, 'Ja – cob.'

The humans did not come that day. At dusk Carl made his way slowly back to his forest litter, feeling saddened and even a little scared at being on his own. Then he remembered Francis. He wished the cat would come by, but Francis failed to appear.

After a while, Carl decided to go and look for him. He felt a very strong desire for company and knew Francis's usual haunts and his favourite trees. But he saw no sign of the cat. Neither did Francis respond to any of Carl's enquiring grunts. There was evidence, however, that he had been around that part of the forest recently. Scraps of bone, skin and feathers dotted the snow under the trees – the remains of recent meals. Carl soon discovered why the cat had moved his quarters.

He heard the sound of eating – a steady crunching noise. Curious, he went towards it. The Rottweiler, with legs widely braced to support himself, was feeding off the remnants of Francis's kills: the dog's injuries had reduced him to chewing the bones of a cat's leavings. Carl paused and watched Roger's movements. They were painfully slow and laborious. His whole demeanour betrayed an extreme weariness. The pig knew he had nothing to fear, but he had been momentarily startled by the dog's presence.

Roger eventually heard the tell-tale snuffles of Carl's ever-active snout. He turned slowly.

'Oh, it's you!' he muttered. 'Surprised you're still here. Have your bleating friends shunned your company?'

Carl did not answer this. Referring to the scraps he said, 'You won't survive long on that sort of food. What are you going to do?'

Roger bared his teeth in a canine grin. 'Perhaps I'll eat you and get my strength back.'

Carl was unmoved; the dog could barely stand. 'You shouldn't have gone hunting the sheep,' he remarked. 'It wasn't worth it in the end, was it?'

Roger looked at him with contempt. 'And what on earth would you know about hunting,' he sneered, 'with your great squat nose only able to root about under others' feet?'

Carl was angry, not at the words, but at the tone of the gibe. He said, 'It seems strange for an animal brought down to such a humiliating level' – he indicated the scraps with his snout – 'to mock the natural habits of one such as myself.'

Roger glowered at him. 'Jacob's going to pay for what he did to me,' he growled. 'My sole reason for eating this detritus' – he spat the word – 'is to enable me to spin out my life long enough to make him regret it!'

'You're living in a dream world,' said Carl. 'Look at you!' But in reality he was alarmed on the ram's behalf by the dog's venom.

'Go away, pig, and don't intrude on me any longer,'

said Roger bitterly. 'I don't need your sort of coun-
selling.'

Carl stepped away without a further word; he had no
wish himself to prolong the interview. Back in his litter he
remained wakeful, wondering about the dog's abilities.
Towards the end of the night he had decided he should
leave nothing to chance; he would have to try and carry a
warning to Jacob of the dog's threats.

At dawn he set off. There had still been no sight of
Francis as Carl left the forest and began his journey over the
melting snow. It was in his mind that the flock could not
have got far away and, since he had some notion of the
direction it had taken, he was quite confident of reaching
it. As the light increased and the air warmed, Carl expected
at each moment to catch a glimpse of the flock in the distance, grazing on the newly uncovered heather. But as he
trundled on without any sign of a single sheep across the
whole landscape, he began to be a little concerned. It was
as if the flock had deliberately gone into hiding.

Some time later Carl stopped dead. He had heard
human cries – faint but unmistakable. His heart began to
beat faster; if only he could find Jacob and pass his
message, he would then be free to give himself up to the
humans. When it became obvious there was quite a
number of different human voices, Carl began to realize
what was happening: the sheep were being sought by a
party of men, and the flock was doing its best not to be
found. Now he was in a real quandary; he had not the
slightest idea where the sheep might have decided to
hide themselves and it might take him an age to find
them, if he ever did. Meantime, the opportunity for
rescue might be lost for good. He stood pondering,
thinking of Roger. Was Jacob really in danger? It was very
unlikely that Roger could kill him in a straight fight;
Jacob would make mincemeat of the dog that way. But

the ram had to sleep . . . . That was the weak point. So, heaving a sigh, Carl continued on his way.

He came to a slight rise in the terrain. At the top, he looked down and saw a motor vehicle parked at an awkward angle on the uneven, slushy ground. He was looking at a Land Rover. To his left, a thicket of dense, spiny blackthorn had shreds and tufts of wool sticking to its branches. Carl knew then that the sheep had been that way. But how long ago?

The next moment he heard a shout and felt himself grabbed. Two men had approached from behind and held him by the legs. He was swung ignominiously into the air and carried away; moments later he was bundled into the Land Rover on to a pile of sacks. Carl's adventures on the moors were over, and Roger's threats were not known to Jacob.

# —16—
# A Death and a Birth

The men had brought dogs in the Land Rover and they soon sensed the presence of sheep. The sheep, of course, sensed the presence of dogs and kept moving. Jacob had not attempted to hide the flock as Carl had supposed; he knew that the best plan was to keep on the move throughout the day, using the vastness of Leckmoor to prevent their being cornered. They spent the night in the thicket where Carl had seen traces of wool, and Jacob, Jess and Asher stayed on guard in turn; at dawn they moved off. They heard the men's voices and smelt the dogs, but the men never caught up with them, and realizing that they had set themselves an impossible task, returned home with one pig, and with a horse and a donkey which they tied by ropes to the back of the Land Rover and allowed to trot behind at a comfortable pace.

Jacob knew when the human pursuers had been shaken off, and only then did he allow a rest and a feed. The sheep were very tired, and nibbled at the exposed heather and brown grass stalks in a desultory way; but there was another pursuer who was able to take his time. He followed the trail of the flock slowly and laboriously, pausing on his splayed legs whenever he felt like it to take his breath or to snatch up a morsel or two. So long as the flock moved he did not come any closer to them; but when they rested he gained ground.

Away from the forest, Jacob began to forget about the Rottweiler. Nevertheless, he still made sure either Asher or Jess was awake when he was not, and eventually Prancer and Dancer begged to be involved. Jacob was in two minds about this, finding it difficult to forget their silly, giddy period of immaturity; but for some time they had shown themselves to be reasonably sensible beasts, and in the end they persuaded him.

As the days went by and the milder weather persisted, gradually the snow retreated altogether and the ground was left sodden and spongy. At last there was food. Small animals began to move around again and occasionally Roger, by standing quite still, was able to lunge at a passing vole or shrew. Sometimes his jaws closed on nothing, at others he was more fortunate. So he managed to survive and, little by little, he closed the gap between himself and the flock. He had no illusions about stealing up on the sheep in the daylight; he knew the darkness was necessary for his plan.

One night the Rottweiler lay down awkwardly by a clump of furze, his mouth running with water as he growled softly in his throat. About fifty metres away he could see the flock: some sheep asleep, others awake. Roger had no plans to advance any further at that stage, satisfied that at last he was within sight of the animals. He scented the fulfilment of his objective and as he thought of Jacob and what he would do to him, his hackles rose. He opened his jaws and panted a little in anticipation. He had come a long way for this and nothing must go wrong now. He allowed himself to doze a while.

After an hour he woke, wondering for a moment where he was. Then, as he sniffed the night air, he remembered; the warm, musty yet sharp smell of sheep wafted on the breeze. He got to his feet with some difficulty and crept forward.

The sheep were sleeping, with Dancer on guard. Dancer looked around, listlessly, bored with the deep silence, his eyelids heavy. He was very drowsy and longed to shut his eyes but dared not. He wondered, idly, if it would matter very much if he lay down; his legs were stiff. Having decided it could not be important whether he stood or lay, gently and noiselessly, so as not to disturb his brother nearby, he lay on the grass. He listened carefully: no, not a sound. His head drooped a bit.

Roger came on carefully, one step at a time. As he neared the flock his eyes began to range over the huddle of woolly bodies, seeking the one particular beast he was after. He saw Myriam, recognizing her as the animal who had acted as a decoy, and his lips curled back over his white fangs in a sardonic grin. Then he spotted Jacob. A growl rose in his throat, but he choked it off.

Dancer's head dropped – he was asleep.

The dog lurched forward awkwardly around the fringe of the flock, trying to see a way through to the big ram who was lying on his side in the centre. He paced this way and that, itching to rush in; but he knew that would be futile. He had no speed now and he would never reach his target that way. He would have to use all his cunning. Curbing his impatience, he crept back into the shadows; Jacob would move and then, once he was standing apart from the rest, he need hesitate no longer. He was close enough now to inflict a surprise attack that would leave Jacob maimed, even if he could not kill him. Roger knew that his own death would inevitably follow shortly after but he cared nothing for that; indeed, he welcomed it. Only his hope of revenge had kept him alive thus far; but he would die knowing that Jacob would never be able to forget him. So Roger hovered in the darkness whilst he ground his teeth.

The entire flock slept but some intuitive instinct told

Jacob something was badly wrong. He awoke suddenly, and saw at once there was no ram standing on guard. He got to his feet and, at once, saw the sleeping Dancer. He was furious. Intending to teach the irresponsible young animal a lesson, he stepped quietly through the flock to where Dancer and his brother lay.

Roger had been watching this in a ferment of excitement. As Jacob stood by the young rams, preparing an almighty bellow of rage, Roger came limping over the intervening ground. Dancer, who had only been drowsing, opened his eyes and jumped up just as Roger lunged at Jacob. Dancer's body took the blow and the Rottweiler's powerful fangs sank into his neck. He fell, with Roger on top of him, the last of his strength used up. Prancer and a dozen other animals were woken to a nightmare scene: the dog, draped over the dying ram like a monstrous cloak; Dancer's throat pouring blood which quickly collected in a dark pool on the spongy ground.

Jacob's roar stuck in his gullet – knowing that the dog had meant this blow to fall on him. Gradually, the life ebbed from Dancer in a warm tide whilst his killer choked out his last breaths on top of him in a ghastly embrace.

By now the whole flock was awake and on its feet, staring in horror at the two carcasses. Becky came silently to Prancer and nuzzled him, as he whispered, 'But why should he want to kill my brother?'

Jacob said, 'Your twin inadvertently saved my life. If only he had stayed watchful he wouldn't have lost his own.'

'I knew we hadn't killed the dog before,' Becky said harshly. 'Now my lamb has paid the penalty.'

'Roger's good and dead now, Becky,' whispered Barley.

'What consolation is that to me and his twin?' the mother snapped.

'There will be more lambs in the spring,' Jacob said gently. 'You'll be a mother again.' His words sounded hollow. He felt guilty although he could not be blamed.

Myriam said, 'I think we should leave this place, Jacob.'

'Yes,' he said. 'We must put all this behind us. Our numbers will grow again, and we must hold on to that.'

'And Jacob's flock will be greater than ever,' chanted Barley.

The sheep were glad to get away from the smell of blood, and the broad sweep of the moors and the cold air of a wintry dawn refreshed them. A group of ponies told Jacob of the capture of Jenny and Captain on the previous day.

'They'll be glad of that,' he said. 'Did the pig go too?'

None of them knew. 'There has been no more hay,' said one. 'But we may not need any more if the snow keeps away.'

'We long for the spring,' said Jacob.

The humans did not return over the next few weeks and the flock relished their freedom. The ewes felt stirrings within them and winter really did seem to have receded. Soon they became aware that others had noticed the arrival of spring; they began to see foxes more frequently, following them at a distance. But they never attempted an attack, nor did they seem to wish to do so. Other predators, too, became more noticeable. Hawks and, occasionally, a raven or two flew overhead, returning again and again as if keeping an eye on the sheep. It was disconcerting to be shadowed by predators and the flock was nervous, but nothing happened. The hawks and foxes were playing a waiting game.

Jacob and Myriam understood these tactics but the

younger rams and ewes were jittery. When they questioned Jacob, he tried to calm their fears without explaining that the predators sensed that the ewes were soon to give birth. He merely told them all never to stray far from the main flock, and that it would be more dangerous than ever before if they did not heed his advice. Needless to say, they listened and obeyed.

At last the ewes began to realize that it was they who were attracting the interest, and they started bleating with fear, wishing that they had been rounded up by the humans and were safe and sound somewhere far away from the foxes.

'Where can we go when our time arrives?' they pleaded. 'How can we protect our young ones from attacks from the air?' They turned to Myriam for advice.

'There is nowhere for you to hide,' she told them honestly. 'You must be vigilant always, never relax for even the briefest moment until your danger is past. But remember, the lambs will not all be born at the same time. There will be plenty of sheep to watch out for each one.'

The days passed. The flock strained every nerve in a constant effort to know where each fox, each buzzard was moving all through the day. The nights were fraught with alarms. Sudden noises: rustlings, distant cries, the crack of a twig or the swish of a brushed plant, were all imagined to be caused by a hovering fox or an owl. Some of the ewes were so tense that they dared not rest. Only the rams, though, discussed the danger.

'We've never faced anything like this before,' said Jess to his father. 'What should we do?'

'Foxes are our main danger,' Jacob told him. 'They're very persistent and we must do all we can to prevent them from approaching too closely.'

'How can we do that?' asked Prancer.

'Do I have to tell you everything?' Jacob boomed irritably. 'How do you think? Use your legs, and your head.'

Later Prancer spoke to Asher alone. He did not like the idea of himself being expected to deal with dangerous, sly creatures like foxes. 'Why do we have to defend the ewes?' he complained. 'We weren't permitted to have anything to do with them when we wanted to. Jacob saw to that.'

'I see your point,' said Asher. 'Jess has Frolic to protect but whom are we supposed to defend? The whole flock?'

'I think that's what Jacob means.'

Asher thought for a moment. 'I don't want to appear cowardly,' he murmured.

'Whatever we do, it will be for Jacob's benefit,' Prancer said quickly as he saw Asher wavering. 'All the lambs will be his progeny, save for Frolic's. My brother lost his life for Jacob and I don't plan to repeat his mistake.'

'I don't know,' said Asher. 'What can we do?'

Prancer could not think of anything persuasive to say so he kept quiet. But he wanted to bring Asher round to his side. He did not want to defy Jacob alone, for he had not yet lost his awe of the old ram.

A couple of nights later Jacob spoke to the young rams again. 'There is a fox who is trying to come closer than before,' he reported. 'It appears to be very determined. We shall have to observe it all the time, and try to drive it off.'

'Could we do that together now?' suggested Asher. 'If it sees what it's up against it might turn tail.'

'We can't go all at once, no,' Jacob answered. 'That might expose the flock to another animal elsewhere.'

'I'll chase it off,' Jess offered confidently, eager as ever to please his father.

'All right, Jess,' said Jacob. 'See what you can do.'

Prancer and Asher watched with mixed feelings as the young ram run off. They did not want any harm to come to Jess but, on the other hand, they felt that if he got himself into difficulties surely Jacob would no longer expect them to encounter foxes alone.

The fox had been lurking near the flock for some days and when no resistance had been offered to its presence it had grown bolder, gradually moving closer. So it was rather taken by surprise when a full-grown ram came charging out of the darkness, head lowered, making straight towards it. It was simple for the fox to take action to avoid confrontation; it loped off out of the ram's path and then returned, bit by bit, on another tack. Jess was ready for this and ran at the fox again, and again the fox used the same tactics. After a few more rushes, Jess began to tire. He realized he was achieving nothing and returned to Jacob.

'He's certainly determined,' he said shortly and, even as he turned to look back, he could see the fox's eyes glowing in the moonlight a matter of twenty metres away.

'You did your best,' Jacob said. 'It's very difficult to dislodge a hungry fox.'

'Is there anything else we can do?' Jess asked.

'No, not for the moment,' answered his father. 'He won't dare to come closer than that as long as we're patrolling around the flock. Let him stay skulking for the time being.'

'But what if hunger should overcome his caution?' Jess queried.

'Yes, there is that possibility. But if he realizes that he

can't get past our barrier, he might see sense and search
for smaller prey.'

'Surely we can't all keep our eyes on that one animal?'
suggested Asher. 'There are other foxes about as well.'

'Of course there are,' said Jacob. 'We're going to have
to station ourselves at different places around the flock.
The ewes will help, too, of course, if any animal attempts
to run in.'

So this became the policy for the succeeding nights.
The flock was kept together in a bunch and around the
edge the rams stood guard. This meant that they needed
to sleep during daylight hours, during which Myriam
organized Frolic and some of the other dependable
females to share the watching with herself.

Early spring saw the first new lamb born safely and
Bridget became the first mother of the season. She was
delighted and very proud of her lamb – a female. Some of
the other ewes tittered and joked among themselves
because Bridget continued her everlasting chewing
throughout the birth, but she cared nothing for that. She
had what she wanted.

The first of the year's births, however, was somewhat
overshadowed by an unexpected occurrence. Some days
after the birth, Jacob, who was grazing a little way from
the other sheep, looked up to see two animals approaching him; a ewe and an extremely young lamb. They came
very slowly because of the youngster's diminutive size,
the mother constantly scanning the countryside for any
danger. It was not until she was quite near to him that
Jacob finally recognized the ewe as being the last animal
he had ever expected to see again – it was Bell.

# The Turning Back

Jacob was astonished; he could only stare at Bell. The lamb kept so close to Bell's side he could have been joined to her: he moved when she moved, stopped when she stopped. When they reached Jacob the little fellow was most inquisitive and sniffed at the great ram, examining his feet and his chest and his tail. He was very curious, but he sniffed at Jacob gingerly, as if he did not know quite what to make of him and should keep himself ready to skip back to his mother in case of doubt. He had appealing eyes and a long fluffy tail and Jacob was enchanted. He knew him for his own and he looked long at Bell. He was glad to see her, and she was aware of it.

'We all thought you were dead,' he said in a low voice. 'All this time, how have you survived? Where have you been, Bell?'

'With Reuben,' she answered simply.

'Reuben? But you were missing when he and his females left us.'

'I joined him later – it seemed to be for the best. I got buried in a snow drift and I couldn't move. I thought it was the end of me but – well, it wasn't.'

'It's good to have you back with my, I mean, our little youngster. He has your looks!'

Bell was pleased with the way things were going,

obviously Jacob's attitude toward her had changed. She
had not known how it would be when she made the decision to return.

'How did you find us?' Jacob asked.

'I asked the ponies. It was a nerve-racking journey, I
couldn't rest for a single moment – foxes and things
everywhere.'

'Why did you come?'

'Of, that's easy,' she murmured. 'Because you're Jacob
and because you're so safe.'

The ram was pleased. 'You risked a lot,' he remarked.

'Yes, but not as much as I would have done if I had
stayed where I was. Reuben tries hard, but he's on his
own – one ram trying to protect a lot of pregnant ewes.
He's no match for the wiles of the foxes. Two of the ewes
gave birth before me and one lamb was snatched before
it had got to its feet. The other was born dead because its
mother had attempted to fend off a buzzard. I was lucky,
but as soon as I could I got away.'

'Poor Reuben,' muttered Jacob. 'It's not so long ago he
was a lamb himself.'

'And your flock?' Bell prompted.

'Oh, yes. We've had our first birth – Bridget's. A long-
tailed little thing like yours.'

'Bridget?' repeated Bell. 'That's ironic.'

'Yes, strange it should be her, but the others are immi-
nent, I think,' Jacob finished awkwardly. 'She's changed,
Bell,' he added as an afterthought. 'I hope you have – I
don't want any discord at a time like this.'

'It certainly won't come from me,' she said. 'I couldn't
be more contented.'

'I think that's how Bridget feels.'

'I'd like to forget the past,' said Bell, 'but is Myriam—'
she broke off hesitantly.

'Oh, you know Myriam,' Jacob said quickly. 'She never

bears a grudge against any creature. She'll be pleased to see you back.'

'I hope you're right,' said Bell. 'Let's go and see.'

Myriam, kindly as ever, showed unfeigned delight at the sight of Bell and her lamb. She listened to her story avidly whilst the other ewes looked on with a mixture of surprise and admiration at Bell's daring, long journey. For just a moment Bridget's face registered resentment, but when she felt her little ewe butting her underside in its desire to feed, the resentment quickly vanished, and she forgot her rivalry.

The safe arrival of Bridget's lamb had made the other pregnant ewes a little more confident and, after hearing Bell's tale, they were doubly glad that they were with Jacob and not Reuben. Jacob himself, though, was very disturbed about Reuben's problems and he wondered if he could help in some way. But this did not seem probable when he had so many females in his own care that he needed to protect.

For a few days the sheep enjoyed without mishap the sweet new shoots of grass that were pushing above the moorland surface. They knew foxes continued to prowl at night and, in the daytime, the wheeling hawks were only too visible. But there was no real alarm since, for this brief spell, there were no further births. Then, as luck would have it, five of the ewes reached their time together. It happened at night.

Jacob knew the signs and hastily organized a sort of screen of females around the ewes who were in labour. Bell and Bridget and their lambs were also behind this shield. Then he, Jess, Prancer and Asher stationed themselves in readiness to repel the attacks of any marauders. Jacob knew he could rely utterly on Jess to do all that was necessary and he was fairly confident that Asher took his duty seriously; but the reliability of Prancer in any real difficulty was very much in question.

Prancer was showing a great deal of nervousness. He was unsettled and jumpy and Jacob hoped that no fox attempted a raid in Prancer's quarter. But the fox who had for days shadowed the flock more closely than any of the others, knew all about this point of weakness and intended to exploit it.

Like all his kind, this beast was an opportunist. He had skulked round the perimeter of the flock often enough to test the old ram's defences; trying a move here, a feint there, and then a charge in a third place. He was perfectly aware that his best chance was to go for Prancer. The fox knew now that the time was ripe, and keeping his eye constantly on Jacob, he slunk over the ground almost on his belly until he was within a few metres of the agitated Prancer. The fox could smell the new lambs and he salivated. He knew other foxes hovered nearby, awaiting their chance, but he wanted to be the first to attack. Prancer could smell the strong musky odour of fox: it seemed to the young ram he was surrounded by the animals and the air smelt heavy with their presence. He twisted and turned about, always trying to see through the gloom where the foxes were lying; what they were doing; if they were moving.

'Steady, Prancer,' Jacob encouraged him urgently, sensing an attack. 'Don't waver. If we can just—'

The rest of his words were lost. A fox rushed out of the darkness, ran round Prancer before the young male realized what had happened, raced between two ewes and had fastened a grip on the helpless newborn animal before the mother or any other sheep could stop it. The fox was so daring and so swift that it was all over as soon as it had begun. As Jacob ran round towards Prancer who now stood stupidly, quivering with fright, more foxes rushed in, striking home their advantage. Jess and Asher tried to head them off and Jacob turned again and charged at one, knocking it flying. But there were simply too many foxes. Three of the lambs were snatched from their despairing mothers' sides and then the horrifying sounds of the foxes fighting amongst themselves for the choicest food reached the ears of the whole flock. Even whilst pandemonium reigned, another Sweetriver lamb came into this savage world and eventually staggered to its feet while Becky, its mother, licked it dry.

There was no comforting the ewes. Only two lambs survived – three taken. The foxes had made off with their share of the innocents, but Jacob knew they would be back.

It was a long time before any sort of order could be brought to the flock. Jacob's old heart was torn by the misery of the dispossessed mothers, as well as his own emptiness. And now Barley began her complaints again.

'Three deaths,' she rasped. 'Three deaths because of Jacob's selfishness!'

The old ram was taken aback. He had done all he could to prevent the tragedy, but in the end the foxes had been too much for him. 'No!' he protested. 'That is not true.'

'It's true all right,' Barley answered him at once, with a new bitter tone to her voice. 'You decided to run from the human helpers – "We don't need the human shield," ' she mocked his words savagely. 'Look where it's brought us – our young ones born into the jaws of foxes.' Barley herself was pregnant and foresaw the same fate befalling her.

'I tried. I did all I could, you know it, Barley,' Jacob spluttered. 'We all wanted to stay on the moors . . . .' his voice petered out.

None of the ewes opened their mouths in support of him. He was stunned.

'Myriam,' he pleaded, 'you know I didn't make the decision alone.'

But for once even his old favourite kept silent. She saw the mothers' distress and she understood their resentment.

It was Jess who tried to restore Jacob's position. 'You forget, Barley,' he said, 'Jacob is trying to protect the whole flock. The other rams have tried to help, but what can any of us do against a pack of determined foxes? Do you think Jacob wanted these attacks?'

'Of course not!' Barley snapped. 'Don't be foolish, Jess. But he's endangered us all by allowing us to face such dangers. How many more lambs must die before he will admit he is wrong?'

'All right, Barley,' Jacob said, sounding calmer now and more resigned. 'I did what I did for the best, but maybe you're right. We're not equipped for this sort of contest; we're too vulnerable.'

'What can we do, Jacob?' Bell asked. 'I came back to what I thought was safety; but it seems there is none any more, not even with you.'

At last Myriam spoke. 'We have to find a way, a place, where the other lambs can be born away from danger. I can think of only one way.' She looked at Jacob to see if he could read her thoughts.

The old ram sighed – all his fine feelings of liberty, command and importance had been destroyed by the realities of the flock's situation. He knew there was only one thing for them to do. 'There is only one way,' he admitted, speaking slowly. 'You must follow me back to the old pastures, back under the wing of humankind.'

'It's the kindest way,' Myriam said gently. 'We have to consider our helpless lambs before ourselves.'

'Yes, of course,' Jacob answered her. 'Neither ram nor ewe could quarrel with that sentiment.'

But Myriam was close enough to Jacob's feelings to know there was regret behind his words. He was old, and there could be no future for an old ram in Man's dominion.

The idea of returning to their home pasture set a buzz of conversation going amongst the ewes. Then Barley said, 'It'll be a slow journey; pregnant females and little lambs don't move quickly, and there will be more births along the way. It's all too late – we should have started before.' She looked at Jacob with real animosity. 'If I lose my lamb,' she told him, 'I shall know where to lay the blame.'

Jacob had had enough criticism. 'You know so much, don't you?' he said angrily. 'But you didn't say a word about this earlier. You liked the thought of staying free on the moors as much as the rest.'

'No, I didn't,' Barley argued, 'but I'm sure my lone voice would not have been heeded anyway.'

'I won't bicker with you,' Jacob said with disdain. 'We're in this situation whether we like it or not, and now we can only do the best we can.'

Barley continued muttering to herself, but she was not the most popular of the sheep and none of the others wished to prolong the squabble.

'We shall go carefully, travelling by day,' Jacob said in a tone of authority, trying to reassert himself. 'We should be safe from interference in the daylight.'

'What about hawks, and ravens?' Barley demanded.

Jacob sighed. 'Yes, Barley, I hadn't forgotten those,' he said wearily. 'But they're not too much of a threat, and then, at night, we'll have to devise a plan to foil the raiders.'

'How can we? There is no such plan,' Barley declared. 'Jess had to admit there was nothing that could be done against foxes acting together.'

'They don't act together,' Jacob said. 'You must have heard them fighting each other.'

'Well, they appear together, and that's the same thing,' she insisted.

'Look, Barley,' Jacob said, 'if you think you have the answer as to how we should proceed, I and, no doubt, all the others too, would be only too relieved to hear it.'

As usual, when challenged in this way, Barley was silent. Jacob waited, looking at her questioningly and then said, 'We'll begin at dawn.'

Becky was the one to raise objection now. 'How can I travel with a newborn lamb?' she asked indignantly. The other new mothers agreed with her.

'You can move as soon as he can take a few paces,' Bell said. 'I did it with mine, and you'll have to. It's more perilous to stay still.'

'Another day then, Becky,' said Jacob, 'and then we go.'

And go they did. After an uneventful day, on the second dawn, Jacob mustered the flock together in order, the weakest and the most vulnerable in the middle. Bridget and Bell found themselves side by side with their lambs between them and they both seemed to find amusement in this after all that had passed between them.

'It seems our fates are bound closely together,' Bell remarked good-humouredly.

Bridget chewed for a while. 'Yes,' she said. 'We'd better be friends, hadn't we? There are more than enough enemies for each of us.'

Jacob walked sedately at the flock's head, every fifty metres or so stopping to see if all was well – then he would continue. Buzzards circled continuously overhead. They progressed only a little way before some of the ewes complained of feeling tired. They could see the edge of the forest on the horizon and although Jacob was frustrated by their slowness he knew there was nothing he could do about it. Looking at the forest, he thought of the pig and the cat, and hoped that Carl was comfortable now wherever he was. He decided he cared little about the cat's future.

When dusk began to fall, the old nervousness and agitation about foxes took hold of the sheep anew. Jacob tried to introduce a feeling of calm by stating that there was no reason for any fox to mount an attack that night, but his intention backfired on him. The ewes knew perfectly well that he was referring to new births, and so those ewes who had not yet reached their time became increasingly alarmed that the foxes were waiting on them. The prospect was a very frightening one. Frolic, who was herself one of these, spoke quietly to Jess. 'I want you to promise me something,' she said.

'Of course, Frolic,' he said willingly and without thinking. 'You can ask anything of me.'

'When my time comes,' she said, 'I want you to be here by my side. There might well be other ewes in the same state but your duty is to me more than any of them. Do you understand me?'

'I believe so,' said Jess.

Frolic did not like his tone. 'You think I'm terribly selfish,' she murmured.

'Aren't all mothers?'

'I suppose so, when it comes to their own offspring,' she admitted. 'But, don't you see, Jess, I want our lamb to survive. You can't blame me for that.'

'I don't blame you,' said Jess. 'But suppose I neglected another, and it was killed. That makes me almost a killer myself.'

But Frolic prompted him. 'Please promise me,' she said.

'How can I?' he beseeched her. 'Of course I promise to see you come to no harm, but I can't remain with you and ignore anything else that might be happening. Another animal could be in very real danger.'

'You said I could ask anything of you,' Frolic reminded him.

'Oh, Frolic!' he wailed. 'I'd be letting Jacob down too.'

'No, you wouldn't. I'm his favourite daughter—'

'Yes,' interrupted Jess. 'And you are going to be the mother ewe of the only lamb in this flock not sired by Jacob.'

His words struck home. Frolic realized this altered her own relationship with the old ram. She looked crest-fallen.

'Now,' said Jess, 'do you see?'

Frolic did see and she did not reply.

The night dragged past and Jacob, Jess and Asher listened for foxes and tried to keep awake. Prancer was no longer permitted to help guard the flock and so he slept during the first dark hours. When he awoke it was still night and rain was falling softly and vertically in the absence of any breeze. Jacob was dozing and Jess and Asher too, were lying down – Prancer could not tell if they slept or not. Again he could smell the unmistakable smell of fox, but he heard nothing and could detect no movement through the raindrops. He guessed the foxes were biding their time and for a moment he felt that the whole flock was in his care. He felt strong and dauntless, but this was only because he was confident there would be no attack. The moment passed and his sense of responsibility was replaced by one of extreme helpless-ness. He went quickly over to Asher – he was asleep. Prancer turned in alarm, then he heard Jess's voice.

'Don't fret, Prancer. You're not expected to do anything.'

The young ram was relieved. But Jess's remark hurt. 'Not expected to do anything,' he repeated to himself. 'Is that how they see me? Am I so useless?' He knew he had not done much to earn respect, especially after the raid of the foxes, and he wondered if there was any way in which he could redeem himself. He would have liked to have been thought a hero or, if not that, at least considered to be wise and cunning. Prancer knew he was dreaming; he was none of these things and never would be. But he could be of some help.

He went over to Jess. 'Look,' he said, 'I know you don't think I'm trustworthy – that's not surprising. Can I persuade you, though, to snatch some sleep? I've slept, so I can watch for you. I'll stay right beside you and if there is anything suspicious I'll wake you.'

Jess considered. He really did want to rest properly, and things were quiet enough. 'All right, Prancer,' he said at length. 'Thanks for the offer. But if anything goes wrong this time, well, Jacob—'

'I know, I know,' Prancer broke in. 'It won't go wrong, I assure you. Please let me do this.'

Jess was touched by Prancer's eagerness to help; he seemed almost desperate to be of use somehow. 'All right,' he said. 'Now, don't forget, at the very first sign—'

'I'll wake you. Yes.' Prancer was delighted.

Jess closed his eyes gratefully and for the rest of the night Prancer listened to the rain. That was all he heard, even the foxy smell was washed away by the freshness of the air. When dawn broke and the flock saw the gathering light with relief, Prancer felt he had achieved something, and he felt happy.

# —18—
# Francis Again

The sheep got very near to the forest that day. There were no longer any foxes trailing them, but a very persistent buzzard tested the flock's defences, dive-bombing the tiny lambs and raking the backs of the ewes with its talons as it soared up after its descent. The bird was powerful and could have grabbed one of the youngsters, but for the taller adult animals who automatically jostled together to protect their lambs. It was a long time before this fierce hawk gave up its attacks.

The flock progressed in fits and starts. It was depressingly slow but the lambs had to suckle and the ewes needed to rest and then, late on in the spring afternoon, the sheep came to a full stop. Two more births were about to take place.

Jacob did not know whether to feel pleasure or exasperation. All he wanted now was to reach his goal, away from the dangers and the hostilities. The flock's brief courtship with freedom was over; let Man take over. But he still felt a twinge of pride every time a new lamb of his blood came into the world.

The flock were now close enough to see individual trees on the edge of the forest, but Jacob had no idea how many more days' journeying were needed to bring them within sight of the home pasture. And now, with these frequent stoppages, all the ewes might give birth before

the flock had reached the protection it sought. Jacob had
to acknowledge to himself that Barley had been right in
one respect: it was an agonizingly slow process. And they
still had all the old difficulties to face – the foxes would be
back at night, having followed their scent. Jacob made
sure that he slept before the night came on.

The sheep had another, more welcome visitor before
the early spring dusk had quite fallen. It was Francis, who
had both heard and smelt their presence near his old
territory.

'I thought I couldn't be mistaken,' he said to Myriam.
'My ears told me there was something very familiar
around.'

'Yes, but there have been some changes, as you can
see,' answered the old ewe.

'Indeed,' said Francis, looking at the new lambs. 'I fear
that you're a sitting target for killers like the Rottweiler.'

'Roger is gone,' Myriam told him at once, and described his death. 'Now foxes are our main concern. At
night they're like shadows flitting around us, heavy
with menace.'

'How do you protect the flock?'

'As best we can,' Myriam replied. 'We've had our
losses, but we're on the move whenever we can be. We
have decided to leave the moors now – it's not a safe
home for young lambs up here.'

'I should think not,' Francis agreed. 'I'm moving on,
too. I don't need the forest any more.'

'Where are you heading?'

Francis gave Myriam a broad, feline grin. 'In the direction of the plumpest mice,' he joked.

'We might see you, then, from time to time,' she said.
'But Francis, take care. You're no match for a fox
either.'

'Don't worry,' he purred. 'They don't meddle with me;

they respect the length of my claws too much. The only disagreement I ever had with a fox resulted in one terrified but unscathed cat and one badly scratched and bleeding fox: I can take care of myself. But, I must admit, I'm relieved to hear that great dog is out of the picture.'

'So are we all,' Myriam said. 'We're not equipped to fight carnivores, so the men must do it for us. At least,' she added fatalistically, 'for those who survive.'

'If you feel I'd be of any use, I could stay around for a time,' Francis offered.

'Of course you'd be of use,' Myriam replied.

'Very well,' said the cat nonchalantly. 'I have to catch something to eat but I'll be back.'

Before night Jacob was awake again and Myriam told him about Francis's offer. 'Very generous of him,' said the ram. 'I'm surprised he showed such interest; he always struck me as being very much a loner.'

'Perhaps he's keen to show off his prowess in a fight?'

'Let him, then,' said Jacob. 'But a tussle with a single fox is not quite the same thing as facing a pack of them.'

During the night there was an uneasy silence. Francis appeared out of it with no warning, as noiseless as the darkness itself. He had killed a rabbit and was feeling pleased with himself. Jacob thought he looked rather smug. 'Have you seen anything?' he asked the cat.

'Yes, plenty,' Francis answered. 'But I think we're ready for them, aren't we?'

'I'm never ready for them,' Jacob answered with irritation, annoyed at the other's ease. He went to make sure that Jess and Asher were prepared. Prancer, although forgotten by Jacob, was ready too, and was determined to play his part.

The foxes were gathering. They did not form in a group; they were independent animals, all of whom had tasted the tender flesh of baby lamb and were greedy for more. They approached from different directions, cautiously, always keeping a sly eye on their competitors. There were four of them – all male. The bold one who had rushed past Prancer previously was once again to the fore, his last success having made him confident the tactics could be repeated. But he did not know that the jittery Prancer was no longer on guard; nor did he know that Prancer's place had been taken by a cat, a smaller but fiercer animal.

The foxes paced round the flock, keeping their distance and looking for a likely opening – the daring fox closer than the rest. The hours-old lambs, most at risk out of the flock, nestled with their mothers, and Jacob stood near them, testing the air with his nose. The older lambs were guarded by Jess and Asher. None of the rams had liked to suggest to Francis what he should do, so he prowled around, moving through the flock from one end to the other and then back again with his characteristic coolness.

Although the daring fox was unable to see Prancer, he smelt the tempting aroma of young lamb, and crept closer to the flock.

Francis spotted him and ceased to patrol; his tail twitched and he uttered a soft throaty growl. As the fox wriggled nearer, Francis's back fur began to rise threateningly, his whole body stiffened and an eerie feline howl sounded from the midst of the tightly-packed sheep.

Although puzzled, the fox was not deterred; he halted momentarily and then continued. Out of the corner of his eye he saw a rival fox, a wild-eyed animal, loping forward purposefully and immediately he accelerated to outpace him. As he did so Francis shot towards him, howling and spitting with a fury that alarmed even the sheep. It was sheer bluff, the fox was far more powerful – but it worked. Francis succeeded in halting him and, with his needle-sharp claws unsheathed, aimed a swipe which tore down one side of the fox's muzzle. With a frightened yelp of pain, he turned tail and ran off to nurse his wound.

Now the cat transferred his attention to the other threatening fox, but Jacob decided that, as the flock's leader, he must not be outshone. He launched himself forward at the same beast and this fox, seeing he was to be attacked on both flanks, bid a hasty retreat. That left the other two.

Jacob's place by the tiny lambs had been taken by Jess, leaving Asher in charge of the others – their defence seemed to be secure. Prancer had noticed how easily the first foxes had given up the fight and he soon realized that to attack the attackers appeared to be the best strategy. Eager to atone for his previous failure, he moved out of the flock without a word to any animal, and singled out the beast he intended to charge. This was a wily old fox who, although a little slower than he had once been, was not to be put off easily by the rash courage of a foolish young ram. He merely side-stepped Prancer's charge and began to close in for the kill.

Prancer now swerved around and ran after the fox from the rear, driving it directly on to the flock. Jacob bleated a warning but Prancer's head was down and he heard nothing. The fourth fox held back to see what would happen . . . .

Jess and Asher stood firm until the old fox was almost upon them. He was snapping right and left to fend the sheep off so that he could reach the lambs. The young rams dashed at him together but he slipped between them and was ready to pounce. He was not quite quick enough. The mother ewes used the only defence they had and ran, calling in alarm for their lambs to follow them. The tiny tottering creatures stuck to their mothers instinctively and it was whilst Jacob, Francis, Prancer, Jess and Asher were all converging on the wily fox to impede his progress that the fourth fox saw his chance! Suddenly he nipped between one of the lambs and its mother, and with a lethal snap of his jaws, brought it down. The ewe bleated her anguish and swung round to try and drive the killer off, but she was powerless; the lamb's neck was broken and the fox was already dragging its young body away. So once more, despite heroic efforts, another lamb had been slaughtered.

Jacob said nothing to Prancer, he was too astonished that the young ram had shown such courage. But when the distraught mother eventually rejoined them, she soon gave vent to her feelings.

'Jacob, Jacob!' she cried. 'How can you allow this traitor to stay amongst us?'

Prancer did not even suspect that he was being referred to; he thought he had done a marvellous job.

'Now steady, steady,' Jacob answered. 'You're upset, naturally, but there are no traitors in the flock. The only villains are those murderous foxes!'

'How can you say that?' the ewe wailed. 'He drove the fox right on to us and I had no choice but to run. My lamb didn't have a chance. If one fox hadn't got him, the other one would. You take it so calmly, Jacob. These are your lambs that are being lost – one by one. Which one will be next?' and she continued to cry her misery.

Myriam tried to soothe her. 'A ram doesn't feel quite the same about a lamb as its mother,' she murmured. 'But Jacob does suffer too; I know him.'

Prancer had finally realized who it was that the ewe was accusing and he just could not believe it – after all he had done! His mouth opened and closed once or twice, but he was simply too astounded to find the words to justify himself.

'All right, Prancer,' said Jacob quickly. 'I know how it was; don't say anything now.'

Prancer gaped, not knowing exactly what Jacob did think of him. It was Jess who gave him solace. He stood close and muttered, 'We can only do our best, can't we? We all tried.'

Meanwhile, Jacob was expressing his gratitude to Francis. 'Things might have been much worse without your help,' he finished. But Francis replied that he did not much like animals of the canine variety himself, and it was no skin off his nose.

The flock tried to settle down. It was unlikely that the foxes would be back, but this latest disturbance and killing made them all anxious about their prospects. The pregnant ewes talked amongst themselves, frightened and hopeless. It seemed to them that losses were inevitable so long as they remained on the moors: there was no guarantee that any of them would be safe.

'How long must all this go on?' Frolic demanded, of no animal in particular. 'Can't we get away from here?'

Myriam spoke to Jacob. 'Somehow or other, we must move more quickly. The flock can't tolerate this dreadful toll on our lambs much longer.'

Jacob was as worried as any of the females. 'If it was left to me, I'd keep moving without rest or grazing until we reached the valley. But even in the valley there would be foxes and, to be completely honest, I can think of no way in which we can keep them off. I've thought about nothing else since they first began to shadow us – you'll know that without my telling you – but sheep are very vulnerable animals. To a great extent we are helpless.'

'Yes, it's true. We are,' Myriam admitted. 'And how can you be expected to have the answer?'

'Our only real defence,' he said, 'is to force the pace tomorrow; to put as much ground behind us as we can, even if some of us are stretched to our limit.'

'It would be the lambs who would suffer most.'

'Yes, I know that, but there is no other way.'

Francis had been wandering about, uncertain whether to go on or stay, and Jacob asked him, 'Where will you live now, Francis?'

'I've decided to search for a hearthside myself,' he joked. 'No, really, the spring has caught up with me and I shall go looking for females. There are none to be found up here.'

'You'll travel more quickly than us, then,' said Jacob. 'You're freer.'

'I might go with you if—'

'We'd be pleased if you did,' Jacob interrupted him, enthusiastically.

'Then it's settled.' And without further ado Francis began washing himself with great deliberation and thoroughness.

The ewes were intrigued by his fastidiousness. By comparison with their unkempt fleeces, the cat's coat appeared to them to be spotless. They watched him with great interest until he curled himself up and closed his eyes.

'He could bring us luck,' Jacob said to Myriam.

'Yes, if only he could persuade the foxes to hunt for rabbits, instead of lambs,' murmured Myriam.

# —19—
# To the Valley

Jacob did try to increase the flock's pace the next day as planned, but there were soon objections from the most recent mother ewes, and they were supported by other females, like Barley, who felt their time coming on. So Jacob gave in, feeling more frustrated than ever; there was nothing he could do. It was for the benefit of these very ewes that he was trying to speed their journey along and he was not going to stand for any more nonsense from Barley. Should she begin again about the lack of protection from foxes – well, just let her try!

So the sheep moved slowly over the moorland, past the forest's edge, and gradually it retreated behind them. They paused to graze the succulent new grass and Francis went off on his own in search of mice and voles. He did not travel with the flock all the time, but repeatedly rejoined them at various stages, after wandering off on a new foray. But as night drew in once more he stayed with them.

There were no further births for a while. The rams and the cat stayed vigilant, but the foxes did not return. Perhaps their recent experiences had made them wonder whether it would be worth their while to do so.

Little by little they neared the head of the home valley, each day taking them a further lap on their return journey. With each day, too, the very young lambs grew stronger, able to move a little faster and for a little longer. Jacob began to feel more confident that things were going somewhat better for them all. During the daytime, they still saw a hawk or two circling overhead, keeping the sheep in view in case of a chance kill. But Jacob knew they could prevent attacks from the air by keeping together; more disturbing was the constant thought that the foxes would eventually come back.

After some days Francis wondered if his presence was required any longer. He said as much to Jacob.

'Of course you must do as you decide,' said the ram, 'but I don't think our dangers are over yet. I've an unpleasant feeling we're going to see more of the foxes.'

'Then I'll remain a while yet,' the cat answered non-chalantly. 'We can still see this through together.'

'I'm very grateful. You know that,' Jacob told him. 'If we could just get off these moors before—' He broke off as he heard a commotion breaking out in the flock. The cause was Jess, who was in a very excited state and came running over with the news that Frolic was about to have her lamb.

'All right, Jess,' said Jacob wryly. 'Keep calm. You'd better stay by her, I can hear her bleating for you.' He looked at Francis. The light was just beginning to fade and rain was falling. 'If those beasts are anywhere nearby, they'll soon know about this,' he said grimly.

'I'll be ready,' said the cat.

As the daylight waned, Jacob, Asher and Prancer strained to see any hint of movement beyond the flock. Jess was very jumpy; he was determined to stick by Frolic, yet he found it impossible to keep still. He fidgeted, shivered, went a few steps one way and then back again – then he went in the other direction. He had not known he would be this agitated when the moment should actually arrive, but he remembered his promise to Frolic and he knew that, if necessary, he would have to defend her and their lamb to the death. He desperately hoped that no other ewe would choose the same time to give birth – so testing both his loyalty to the flock and to Frolic. He went back again and eventually was able to watch the tiny, helpless creature that he had fathered taking its first feed from its mother. Somehow the sight of this calmed Jess and he settled down.

Luck was on his side; Frolic's was the only lamb to be born that day. There were no alarms and, by the morning, Jess, and Jacob too, considered that the foxes might no longer be following the flock. They had neither seen nor heard a sign for a few days. Frolic herself was delighted. She was sure her lamb, a little male, would survive, and so now she could afford to be less selfish. She spoke to the other nervous ewes who had not yet given birth, telling them they should be encouraged by the absence of predators. 'I think we've had our worst times,' she said to them brightly. 'We surely must reach our old pasture soon and then how secure and happy we shall all feel!'

Barley refused to be encouraged, it was in her nature to carp and she was true to her nature now, even though all the other ewes wanted so much to believe in what Frolic had said. 'Oh, I expect you're feeling very pleased with yourself,' she said to Frolic. 'All's safe and sound for you. But we've got a long way to go yet and a lot can happen in that time.'

'Why can't you ever look at things from the bright side?' Frolic remarked wearily.

'Quite right,' said Bell. 'It's been one moan after another from you for as long as I can remember.'

Some of the other ewes joined in, in support of Frolic. They really had had enough of Barley and were quite fed up with her.

'You might think I'm always complaining, but I've often been proved right,' Barley answered, defending herself. 'And I've got a feeling that all's not going to go well when it comes to my turn to lamb.'

'She would have,' a number of the females muttered to each other.

Later in the day the flock were able to move on a little way. Jess was anxious about Frolic and their youngster, but she assured him she was ready to travel on. She wanted to make up for her earlier selfishness. Barley kept herself towards the rear, feeling herself misunderstood. She was finding the travelling difficult too, slow as it was, and she knew what this meant for her. Her moment was soon to arrive.

There were, as usual, many pauses for rest and feeding. Then, in the late spring afternoon, Barley became a mother. She had been correct that all was not going to go well for her, but it was nothing to do with foxes – she had a difficult birth. Her lamb was a big one and it was black, the first black sheep ever born into the Sweetriver flock.

None of the others had ever seen a black sheep, and they did not know what to make of it. Even Jacob, with all his years, was puzzled. They stood around Barley, gazing at the little creature, their faces showing astonishment. Some of the ewes began to look from the lamb to Jacob, then at Barley, and then back to Jacob again, doubting that he had indeed sired this youngster. Barley sensed this, but she was at a loss for an explanation herself. She felt a rush of strong motherly emotions for the little lamb as she began to lick its body dry, and as she saw the other sheep continuing to stare at her, she began to feel resentful. 'Here's a fine son you've presented me with,' she said to Jacob. 'And all you can do is stare.'

Jacob turned his back on her and stalked off – this ewe was the end! She did nothing but complain.

Now Barley became defensive. 'I don't know what you're all gawping at!' she snapped at the others angrily. 'It's a lamb. Haven't you ever seen one before?'

Myriam could see how it was. As the other sheep moved away she said kindly, 'All this fuss. It's just a little lamb like all the rest. You must ignore the others, Barley, we were all just a bit curious. You should be proud of such a fine big lamb.'

Barley did not answer and Myriam decided she had better be left to herself. She would soon adjust to her situation. She went away and spoke to Jacob. 'You can be of help to her,' she told him.

'Can I? She's never of any help to me,' he retorted.

'Be patient, Jacob. We all know how awkward Barley can be, but after all, the little creature's yours as well. You've got to make it welcome in the flock and then she'll soon forget her differences.'

'Of course it's welcome,' Jacob answered her. 'All new lambs are welcome in this flock.'

And time passed. The flock continued towards the valley and the little black lamb grew and became sturdier than his contemporaries. Soon Jacob had a feeling of pride whenever he looked at him. There were more births, mostly ewe lambs. Progress was still slow but, with the absence of predators, confidence was restored and at last they came to the limestone outcrop where their moorland wanderings had begun so many months before. Below it the land shelved down. They had reached the head of their home valley.

To Jacob it seemed a momentous occasion. He had sometimes doubted if they would ever see it again and, until the births had begun, he had not desired to. But since the decision to return had been taken, he had longed for this moment and now the valley had come to represent a haven from the wildness. It had been a long, slow trek and there was still a good way to go to their own pasture, but the worst of the journey was behind them. He stood, looking down the valley. Francis was sitting by his side: he had never left them.

'I seem to be looking at my past life when I look down there,' Jacob remarked to him, almost wistfully.

'I know this place too,' said the cat. 'I came this way, to escape the water.'

'So did we all,' Jacob reminded him. 'Do you think it will still be there?'

'I don't know. It was moving so fast it could be anywhere by now.'

'We must find the place where we were pastured; then the lambs will be cared for.'

'We're both looking for something we left behind,' Francis said. 'I wonder if we'll find it?'

'Oh, we're sure to,' said Jacob. But in reality he was not sure at all.

The flock grazed contentedly around the rocks. Most of the older sheep recognized the landmark and knew its significance – there were still many lambs to be born and they were lucky to have arrived at a more peaceful place.

In an hour or so the whole flock was moving down the valley. They passed the place where Frolic had fallen into the chasm and the very sight of it made her shudder. She made sure her lamb was well away from any danger. The sheep did not get much farther that day and dusk was falling as Francis left them. He had seen signs of rabbits earlier and he wanted to catch one.

For the first time in many days Jacob felt safe in allowing all the animals to sleep at once. An air of calm and quiet pervaded the valley and the animals, for so long tense and wary, were at last able to relax. The nocturnal hours slipped past uneventfully, but before dawn there was a rude awakening for all of them.

A frightened, piercing feline cry, rather like a scream, was heard nearby, and, a moment or two later Francis shot towards them. His ears were laid back and he was running at full stretch. Close on his heels was a fox, and the fox's much longer legs and stride allowed it to gain on the cat rapidly. Francis did not stop as he came up with the flock, but raced on past, in desperate search for a tree. But there were none at all in the vicinity and he ran blindly on, vainly looking for some other object to climb.

Jacob and several others of the sheep got up hurriedly when they saw the fox, but this beast showed no interest in the flock's presence. It appeared to be intent only on catching Francis. After the first alarm at the sight of the fox, Jacob quickly realized that the cat was in great danger and that he needed help. There was no use his giving chase too – he could not hope to match the swiftness of either of these smaller animals – but he knew that Francis had stayed to help the flock in their time of danger, and now he had a right to expect them to come to his aid in return. But what on earth could they do?

Jacob could still see the poor cat running this way and that, altering his course and doubling back in a furious effort to shake off his pursuer. But the fox was equal to these manoeuvres and hardly seemed to lose ground at all. The ram could stand still no longer. 'Come on, Jess. Come on, Asher,' he bellowed. And he broke into a lumbering sort of run, in the wake of the chase. The other rams followed him, and Prancer followed them without being asked.

It was not long before Francis, having veered off on another tack, now approached in their direction again and Jacob knew that this was his opportunity to do something. He looked quickly round and saw the three young rams close behind him. 'Go for the fox,' he told them grimly, and lowered his head.

The fox soon saw that four large sheep were bearing down on him and he pulled up abruptly, allowing Francis to get well away. He was not at all afraid, only surprised. He knew he could easily outrun these cumbersome, woolly creatures but he stood his ground, puzzled. Why were they coming to attack him? When Jacob was so close that the fox had to move, the animal darted away, but not to a great distance. Then it stood and watched. The other rams gradually slowed down and then looked about them, uncertain of what to do next.

'I'm over here, sheep,' the fox called cheekily. 'I don't know what you want with me?'

'Just keep away from all of us,' Jacob called, trying to make his voice sound stern, though he was gasping noticeably.

'Have no worries on that score,' the fox replied. 'I'm no sheep lover – and for good reason,' he added to himself.

Jacob stared at him. He thought he had come across this animal before somewhere, though not on the moors. He searched his memory.

Then the fox himself said slowly, 'I know you, don't I? Yes, we met. Now where was it? Round about here . . . I'm sure of it. Before the winter.'

Now Jacob remembered. This was the young fox who had had a tussle with Reuben and had later led the old ram to the gulley and to Frolic.

'Yes, I remember you,' Jacob answered him. 'You did me a good turn once, after a fashion.'

'Well, do me one,' said the perky young fox. 'Tell me where you've been and why you ran at me.'

'We've been on the moors,' Jacob told him, 'right

though the winter. Now we're returning home. It's lambing time, and we need protection.'

'From the likes of you!' Prancer cried boldly, guessing
that he had nothing to fear from this character with the
glossy coat.

'I've told you,' the fox said. 'I don't go in for sheep killing; rabbits and the like are less trouble, so why the
aggression?'

'We've had a stomachful of foxes and their nasty sly
ways,' Jacob said evenly. 'And the cat's our friend.'

'Is he? I can't think why. He stole my supper from me,
or tried to, so I chased him. Thought I'd teach him a
lesson – and I would have done, too, if you hadn't
cropped up!'

'Well, let's leave things as they are, shall we?' Jacob
said, and started to move away. 'There's been no harm
done to any of us.'

'I'll tell you something for nothing,' the fox called after
him. 'You'll find a few changes on your way. This is my
patch all around here so I know what I'm talking
about.'

But Jacob was not listening any more. He wanted to
know what had happened to Francis.

# —20—
# Strange Country

Francis had buried himself in the woolly heart of the flock, as if he regarded the tightly packed bodies as a sort of substitute forest. Jacob was pleased to see him and consoled him at once with the news that the fox had gone his way.

'So you tried to pinch his meal?' he asked the cat jovially.

Francis was not amused. 'Is that what that creature told you . . . well, that's a fox's way, isn't it? I caught the rabbit and this impudent beast came coolly along and tried to grab it from in front of my nose. After all the stalking I had done! When I objected he didn't like it and decided to drive me away.'

'Well, at least you're in one piece, Francis,' said Jess. 'You nearly made the fox a second meal.'

'Thanks for your help,' Francis muttered, adding unconvincingly, 'of course, I would have slipped him in the end anyway.'

None of the sheep replied to this.

'Well, I'm famished,' the cat remarked. 'I didn't get a single bite.'

'Why don't you go back and retrieve the rabbit?' Asher suggested in mock innocence.

'Well, no, it's a long trek, and I'm tired out,' Francis

answered hurriedly. 'I'll rest a bit and then catch a mouse or two.'

'Whilst the fox enjoys your rabbit,' Asher murmured wickedly.

Francis pretended not to hear, and began his complicated washing ritual to conceal his embarrassment.

When day broke, the homeward journey continued. Four more ewes, who had grown to be amongst the biggest in the flock, now reached their time, and each gave birth to a set of twins. It seemed as if the twin births were all going to take place towards the end of the lambing. Myriam was still waiting, and she began to wonder about herself – she had never produced two lambs together. But whatever hers was to be this time, she was quite sure it would be her last delivery. She had lived through many seasons and this would be her final lambing.

Jacob's stout old heart swelled as his eyes roved over the lambs. The flock was growing and the losses were replenished. Oh, but how he wished Reuben, Snow and the rest of them were included in the numbers, making the Sweetriver flock complete. He supposed he would never know what would happen to them.

He watched the black lamb with amusement as he urgently butted at his mother in his desire to feed. She stood patiently, legs apart, whilst he suckled hungrily and Jacob had to admit that Barley had proved to be a model mother, after her initial indignation. She guarded her lamb jealously, kept him near her always and, since his arrival, had become so calm and quiet that it was difficult sometimes to recognize the bad-natured ewe of the past.

The next few days brought more lambs into the flock, mostly twins, and again progress was very limited. Nevertheless, Jacob led them as far as the burnt fields which they had crossed the previous summer.

The ashy blackness which had alarmed him so much then, had given way to a film of new, green growth which sprouted above the surface. Rain, snow, frost and wind had broken down and dispersed most of the remnants of the burnt stubble; but traces of it could still be seen beneath the green shoots and so Jacob knew they were on the right course.

With a gladness almost as great as that of seeing a wandering sheep return to the flock, Jacob saw and recognized the lone rock near the burnt wheatfields. But it was to be the last feature that would appear so familiar in the landscape as he sought for their particular home pasture.

They crossed the altered fields where Jacob had once, as a young ram, been put to graze. Then below them the solitary rock stood out as plain as a beckoning finger. The flock rested and nibbled at the vegetation. Some of the sheep, especially the mothers, wanted to know how much longer their journey would last. Jacob was optimistic.

'When we've passed the rock, which you'll remember from before, there can only be one day or, perhaps, two days' more travelling – that's unless your companions choose to increase our numbers on the way.' The ewes, for the most part, had not remembered the rock; they generally paid little attention to such things. But they were delighted that, at long last, they were close to their journey's end. Now all that they wanted was to get there just as quickly as possible so that their lambs might grow strong and healthy under the comforting control of the humans. None of them thought beyond that: they had no reason to do so.

Jacob himself and Myriam understood something of what the future entailed as far as they were concerned.

Neither of them, in all their seasons, had ever witnessed a sheep's death through old age. They knew that when an animal became particularly elderly or unhealthy it would be removed from the flock and since they were both elderly they had no illusions about what they themselves were returning to. Jacob was content to have done what was best for the flock and its youngsters, realizing that his own days were numbered as, too, were Myriam's. But they were both quite resigned. After Myriam had given birth the breeding days would be over for them and they accepted that that meant their lives were as good as over, too.

Whilst the flock settled down as darkness fell, the two of them spoke together.

'I don't think I shall see another winter,' Jacob confessed.

'It might be so. Who knows?' Myriam answered him. 'But the flock will survive, and when you're gone your blood will still be in every one of those sheep. Jacob will continue in the flock.'

'A comforting thought,' he said. 'And what a comfort it would be, too, if we are on the home pasture when your lamb arrives.'

'Each new day I think it must be the day,' Myriam said. 'But somehow it passes like the one before.'

'Ram or ewe, your lamb will be my favourite,' Jacob declared. 'It might be another Reuben.'

'Yes,' she sighed, reminded of Reuben, wandering the moors with his flock.

Francis joined them. 'I think tomorrow will see our taking separate paths,' he said. 'We're close now to what each of us seeks.'

Jacob said, 'I'm very glad that our paths have run side by side for so long.'

'I feel the same,' said the cat. 'We both have reasons to

be thankful for each other's help in a tight corner.'

'Will you ever return to the moorland?' Myriam asked him.

'No, Myriam, like all of you I came to the moors almost by chance. They were at the end of our escape route and I don't think those circumstances will ever be repeated.'

'Do you remember Carl?' Jacob asked.

Francis said, 'Yes – a comical creature, wasn't he? Wherever he is now, I hope he's more content.'

'Apart from a more agreeable temperature, I don't think he wanted much really,' Jacob said with a far-off look. He was trying to picture the forest. 'I believe he quite enjoyed our society.'

When dawn broke all the flock knew they were on the last lap. There was a feeling of light-heartedness amongst the animals, spreading from Jacob downwards throughout the flock so that the lambs skipped and danced though they did not know why, and the older ones would have played together if they had been permitted to.

For a while they moved along happily in their usual formation – three or four abreast, the lambs in the middle and Jacob up front with Myriam, Jess and Francis. Asher and Prancer walked to the side on either flank. Myriam noticed Jacob exchange a look with the cat once or twice, as if each was waiting for the other to break away, but they kept on together. Then Francis ran on ahead a little way. Myriam thought then that he would leave them, but he merely paused and sat down, turning his head this way and that. At the same time Jacob began to feel a little puzzled: he had expected by now to have seen signs that they were nearing the countryside that surrounded the high pasture they had left during the flood, but there were no signs – at least not obvious ones. And yet he felt instinctively that they were going the right way.

Francis ambled back to the head of the flock. 'This is rather odd,' he remarked. 'We must be coming by a different route after all. I thought I remembered some of it before, but I must have been mistaken.'

Jacob was struck by the way the cat's words echoed his own thoughts. 'But it is the same route we came on before, I'm certain of it,' he said, 'although somehow it doesn't look right at all. I wonder if I've gone the wrong way somewhere?' He was beginning to look rather troubled.

'Don't worry, Jacob,' Myriam said kindly. 'We're so close now it can't make much difference. We won't have gone much out of our way.'

The flock continued to move in fits and starts. It was obvious to all the sheep that Jacob was in a quandary, continually stopping to gaze about in rather a baffled way. He had never expected to find any difficulty in locating the old pasture, he thought it would simply be a matter of knowing the old landmarks – a tree here, a thicket there, a stream or a knoll. These features Jacob had seen day after day all through the summer, but they did not seem to exist any more. It was as if the old limited world of his piece of the landscape had moved away somewhere else, leaving a strange stretch of countryside to replace it. But there was one thing Jacob was certain they had to do, no matter what – it was to continue to descend the valley, to move always in the direction of lower ground. Soon they must strike what they were aiming for.

Francis, who was far more clever than any sheep, had an inkling of the reason for their feelings of disorientation. He had been looking very hard for a particular small building which would confirm whether he was on the right track. This was a dilapidated old barn, no longer used by Man, and before the flood he had many times taken shelter in it during his nocturnal wanderings. Now suddenly, Francis saw the small remnant of it that had not been torn down by the raging waters, and despite the barn's different appearance the cat knew it for what it was. The ruin now stood where the old barn had once, and Francis recognized it.

Jacob saw him walk all round this battered object, sniffing carefully. He assumed that the cat had left them now, and the flock passed on by. As the sheep descended further they passed the spot where their master had last pastured them but none of them recognized the scene of devastation. On their right a stream ran busily downhill – one of the Leck River's tributaries whose course had been changed by the differences in the lie of the land.

The slow journey was an adventure for the little, long-tailed lambs who had never seen any of the places before. They did not know where they were going nor what the old ram was looking for. The adult ewes and young rams wandered obediently on in Jacob's wake, never really questioning his ability to get them back. Even Barley, who at one time would have had a lot to say about his air of bewilderment, now held her peace. She was content simply to be one of the followers.

Francis appeared again, abruptly, by Jacob's side. 'I think I know what has happened,' he murmured.

Jacob looked at him sharply. 'What do you mean?'

'This seems like strange country, doesn't it?'

'Yes,' said Jacob, 'but I'm hoping that soon I shall—'

Francis cut him off. 'You won't "soon" anything,' he told him crisply. 'It has all changed. It's no good expecting to find our old lives again; they disappeared with the flood.'

'The . . . flood?' muttered Jacob.

'Don't you understand? All that power, the water, it changed things.'

'I remember the water,' said Jacob grimly. 'We had to

escape it; it was trying to cover everything.'

'Yes, yes, it covered the area and took most of it away!'

Jacob was beginning to see what Francis was getting at. 'Then our pasture . . .' he murmured.

'Gone!' cried Francis.

'And the buildings, the master's home?'

'Gone too.'

'But what do we do then? Where will you go, Francis?'

'I don't know. I shall explore further, over that way, where I went just now. Will you go back to the moors now?'

'Oh no!' cried Jacob. 'How could we, after all we suffered up there? We shall just have to keep moving, down the valley until we . . .' he paused, unsure of himself.

'Until you find help?'

'That's it,' Jacob said. 'Human help for the lambs. There must, I suppose, still be humans around?'

'Of course,' Francis assured him. 'They're always around somewhere. Well, go carefully, Jacob.'

'I shall. Good luck; I hope you find what you want.'

The cat walked away in his graceful fashion as if he had all the time in the world and Jacob watched him for a while. The flock had begun feeding, so he bent his own head and nibbled gladly at the succulent young herbage. They had to eat and, while they ate, perhaps some humans would find them.

But they were not discovered, and soon they were on the move again. The lambs had all suckled and were feeling strong and lively and now that the adults were refreshed too, Jacob's pace increased. He did not stop any more but walked straight on. He began to trot down the steeper inclines, and soon they had reached the valley bottom, where the land dipped down into the outskirts of the village of Sweetriver itself.

It was late afternoon on a fine spring day as Jacob led the flock down a steep lane and past the first cottage on the edge of Sweetriver. For a while nothing unusual was noticed by the villagers. But as the sheep progressed further, funnelling two abreast through a narrow foot-path between two buildings, they were spotted by an old woman from her bedroom window. She watched them in amazement but, since she lived alone and had no near neighbours, their arrival in the centre was quite un-heralded.

Jacob halted at last. The noise and bustle of the few vehicles and late shoppers disconcerted him and the flock milled about in the road uncertainly, not knowing whether to turn back or press on. Finally Jacob moved off in the direction of the sea front, the flock stepping ner-vously but faithfully behind him. People stopped and stared, gesticulating and calling to each other. But none of these was competent to take charge – so the animals went on.

At last, near the little harbour of Sweetriver, a farm worker, strolling to a tobacconist's, came face to face with the flock. He recognized Jacob at once, despite all the changes wrought in his appearance by the last seven or eight months on the moors and in the forest. The man ran at once to telephone Mr Talbot who had been stay-ing with a friend, another farmer, since he and his wife had become homeless.

About half an hour afterwards a car jerked to a halt on the sea road. Talbot and his dog Kep got out of it and ran towards the harbour and the sight of Jacob and his other sheep, dirty, lean, dishevelled and with long unkempt fleeces, came as if in a dream to the sheep farmer. He saw the little lambs with their long unclipped tails and saw those that had been lambs before the flood and were now fully grown, though he did not recognize them individually. He saw a few pregnant ewes, amongst them grizzled old Myriam. And when he looked at Jacob, his once massive ram, who had kept the flock together all these long months, he almost wept. How was it they had come here, to the village, on this spring day, just as if they had never disappeared at all? It was a miracle.

Jacob and the others at the front of the flock saw Kep and Talbot with their own feelings of surprise and gladness.

'Kep's alive,' Jacob murmured to Myriam wonderingly. 'She's alive and – now we shall get home.'

Kep held her peace: a sheepdog waiting for her master's command. Then Talbot gave it, and she got alongside and then to the rear of the flock and began to drive them along the road, out of the village. A small crowd of delighted onlookers gathered to see them go. The sheep went over the makeshift bridge that had replaced the one torn down by the flood, then on, slowly, while traffic halted to let them pass. Talbot walked behind, cradling the black lamb. On an impulse he had plucked the little creature from the mass of animals, in a desire to look at him more closely. Barley ran by his side, bleating her protests vehemently.

The sheep were being driven to Talbot's friend's farm, where a vacant paddock was to be their temporary accommodation. The man was a dairy farmer and really only had room for the sheep as a short-term measure. In the suddenness of the flock's arrival he and Talbot had had no time to talk about what might be done with them.

Talbot had soon counted his adult animals and realized that the flock was far from complete – he would have been quite astounded if it had been. The sheep had put on weight over the recent weeks of grazing the first shoots of spring grass, but, to the farmer's eyes, they were poor-looking and lean. Before anything else they needed to be fattened up, but he knew he could not expect his neighbour to allow them pasture for long as the man had turned his prize bull out of the field especially for their reception. This needed some thinking about.

When the flock had arrived safely in the paddock and the gate had been closed behind them, Kep's work was done. Darkness was stealing across the farm. Then, as if the old ewe had been waiting for such a restful moment all along, Myriam bleated, knowing her time to give birth had at last arrived.

Her lamb was beautiful, a single, healthy female. It was the most perfect lamb, thought Myriam, that she had ever produced.

# Epilogue

# 'The Sheep who Returned Home'

'This is the end,' Jacob said. 'Now there will be no more travelling.'

Most of the members of the flock were glad; they wanted only abundant food which could be eaten in peace and protection, whilst their lambs grew big enough to graze alongside them. But there was a wistful note to Jacob's voice, as if he regretted in part the return to their owner's control. In fact he did hanker for some aspects of their old life on the moors, in the forest and on the move – free and unfettered.

'But this isn't home,' Barley pointed out, referring to the paddock. 'You'll feel differently when we're back in our own pasture.'

'It's as much home as our old pasture,' Jacob told her. 'Where Kep is and the master, there is a home for us: the comfortable, controlled sort of home which you all wanted again.'

'It's better like this,' Myriam said. 'I know that my lamb is safe. I'm only sorry for those ewes whose lambs were taken from them.'

'They'll breed again,' commented Bridget, between chews. 'You can't expect to be a mother every season.'

'They'll breed again, yes,' Jacob said to himself. 'But – I won't be here to see it.'

The two farmers had been discussing the sheep and

Talbot found he was in difficulties. His friend had agreed without reservation to allow the flock to stay until the lambing was completed, and the local veterinary surgeon had already been requested to come and examine those born in the wild, and give his opinions as to the health and condition of the flock as a whole. But Talbot knew that eventually he would have to face the choice of selling the animals or slaughtering them. Neither of these prospects appealed to him: he would make next to nothing on a sale and how could he bring himself to send them to their deaths after all they had suffered? Besides, more importantly, they had shown a sort of loyalty to him by returning home. He just did not know how he would be able to decide.

A good number of people in the village, however, had witnessed the Sweetriver flock's walk through the streets, and this caught the public imagination. When the flock's identity was confirmed, word spread around about 'the sheep who had returned home' and as time went by they came to represent to the villagers the struggle for survival which had taken place after the flood – they became a symbol of endurance. Once Talbot and his wife were aware of the new stature enjoyed by their animals it became quite unthinkable that they should be destroyed or removed from the locality. But they could not continue to presume on the good neighbourliness of the other farmer, so what could be done?

At last a solution appeared. A sympathetic local landowner offered the sheep pasturage for as long as desired so that 'the flock who had returned home' need not be split up. The sheep's owner was overwhelmed.

As soon as practicable the whole flock, lambs and all, were moved. They really had become something of a curiosity by now and people from all around travelled to look at them. Jacob, the old ram, was a celebrity. More than the other animals, he had to get used to being an object of interest, and he was never able to discover why.

But he did discover one thing. The landowner whose grass they were all permitted to enjoy was an animal lover and had already provided home for another dis-possessed beast: Carl the pig. From his yard he had seen the flock arrive, and so eager had he appeared to be to get through his gate to mingle with them, that he had been allowed to roam the adjoining field where the sheep were pastured.

'Well, well,' he said cheerfully, 'I never thought to see all of you again.'

His friends, too, were delighted to see him and Jacob and the pig exchanged their news.

'I thought you'd had enough of the tame life of the farm,' said Carl.

'Well, you see, Carl,' Jacob explained, 'it's really that the ewes had had enough of the wild life of the moors.'

'I understand. So you came back.'

'Yes, but Reuben went his own way and some of the ewes followed him. I will always wonder if they are still there.'

*Other great reads* from **Red Fox**

Further Red Fox titles that you might enjoy reading are listed on the following pages. They are available in bookshops or they can be ordered directly from us.

If you would like to order books, please send this form and the money due to:

ARROW BOOKS, BOOKSERVICE BY POST, PO BOX 29, DOUGLAS, ISLE OF MAN, BRITISH ISLES. Please enclose a cheque or postal order made out to Arrow Books Ltd for the amount due, plus 22p per book for postage and packing, both for orders within the UK and for overseas orders.

NAME _____

ADDRESS _____

_____

*Please print clearly.*

Whilst every effort is made to keep prices low, it is sometimes necessary to increase cover prices at short notice. If you are ordering books by post, to save delay it is advisable to phone to confirm the correct price. The number to ring is THE SALES DEPARTMENT 071 (if outside London) 973 9700.

*Other great reads* from **Red Fox**

## Discover the great animal stories of Colin Dann

### JUST NUFFIN

The Summer holidays loomed ahead with nothing to look forward to except one dreary week in a caravan with only Mum and Dad for company. Roger was sure he'd be bored.

But then Dad finds Nuffin: an abandoned puppy who's more a bundle of skin and bones than a dog. Roger's holiday is transformed and he and Nuffin are inseparable. But Dad is adamant that Nuffin must find a new home. Is there *any* way Roger can persuade him to change his mind?

ISBN 0 09 966900 5   £1.99

### KING OF THE VAGABONDS

*'You're very young,' Sammy's mother said, 'so heed my advice. Don't go into Quartermile Field.'*

His mother and sister are happily domesticated but Sammy, the tabby cat, feels different. They are content with their lot, never wondering what lies beyond their immediate surroundings. But Sammy is burningly curious and his life seems full of mysteries. Who is his father? Where has he gone? And what is the mystery of Quartermile Field?

ISBN 0 09 957190 0   £2.50

*Other great reads* from **Red Fox**

## THE WINTER VISITOR   Joan Lingard

Strangers didn't come to Nick Murray's home town in winter.
And they didn't lodge at his house. But Ed Black had—and Nick
Murray didn't like it.

Why had Ed come? The small Scottish seaside resort was
bleak, cold and grey at that time of year. The answer, Nick
begins to suspect, lies with his mother—was there some past
connection between her and Ed?

ISBN 0 09 938590 2   £1.99

## STRANGERS IN THE HOUSE   Joan Lingard

Calum resents his mother remarrying. He doesn't want to move
to a flat in Edinburgh with a new father and a thirteen-year-old
stepsister. Stella, too, dreads the new marriage. Used to living
alone with her father she loathes the idea of sharing their small
flat.

Stella's and Calum's struggles to adapt to a new life, while
trying to cope with the problems of growing up are related with
great poignancy in a book which will be enjoyed by all older
readers.

ISBN 0 09 955020 2   £1.95

*Other great reads* ✎ *from* **Red Fox**

**The Millennium books are novels for older readers from the very best science fiction and fantasy writers**

## A DARK TRAVELLING   Roger Zelazny

An 'ordinary' 14-year-old, James Wiley has lost his father to a parallel world in the darkbands. With the help of his sister Becky, James, the exchange student and Uncle George, the werewolf, James goes in search of his parent.

ISBN 0 09 960970 3   £2.99

## PROJECT PENDULUM   Robert Silverberg

Identical twins Sean and Eric have been chosen for a daring experiment. One of them will travel into the distant past. The other into the distant future. And with each swing of the time pendulum they will be further apart . . .

ISBN 0 09 962460 5   £2.99

## THE LEGACY OF LEHR   Katherine Kurtz

The interstellar cruiser *Valkyrie* is forced to pick up four sinister, exotic cats, much to the captain's misgivings. His doubts appear justified when a spate of vicious murders appear on board.

ISBN 0 09 960960 6   £2.99

## CHESS WITH A DRAGON   David Gerrold

The Galactic InterChange was the greatest discovery in history . . . but now it had brought disaster. Unless Yake could negotiate a deal with the alien in front of him, mankind would be reduced to a race of slaves.

ISBN 0 09 960950 9   £2.99

*Other great reads* ⤳ *from* **Red Fox**

**Haunting fiction for older readers from Red Fox**

## THE XANADU MANUSCRIPT
John Rowe Townsend

There is nothing unusual about visitors in Cambridge.

So what is it about three tall strangers which fills John with a mixture of curiosity and unease? Not only are they strikingly handsome but, for apparently educated people, they are oddly surprised and excited by normal, everyday events. And, as John pursues them, their mystery only seems to deepen.

Set against a background of an old university town, this powerfully compelling story is both utterly fantastic and oddly convincing.

'An author from whom much is expected and received.'
*Economist*

ISBN 0 09 9751801   £2.50

## ONLOOKER   Roger Davenport

Peter has always enjoyed being in Culver Wood, and dismissed the tales of hauntings, witchcraft and superstitions associated with it. But when he starts having extraordinary visions that are somehow connected with the wood, and which become more real to him than his everyday life, he realizes that something is taking control of his mind in an inexplicable and frightening way.

Through his uneasy relationship with Isobel and her father, a Professor of Archaeology interested in excavating Culver Wood, Peter is led to the discovery of the wood's secret and his own terrifying part in it.

ISBN 0 09 9750708   £2.50

*Other great reads* from **Red Fox**

## AMAZING ORIGAMI FOR CHILDREN
Steve and Megumi Biddle

Origami is an exciting and easy way to make toys, decorations and all kinds of useful things from folded paper.

Use leftover gift paper to make a party hat and a fancy box. Or create a colourful lorry, a pretty rose and a zoo full of origami animals. There are over 50 fun projects in Amazing Origami.

Following Steve and Megumi's step-by-step instructions and clear drawings, you'll amaze your friends and family with your magical paper creations.

ISBN 0 09 9661802   £4.99

## MAGICAL STRING   Steve and Megumi Biddle

With only a loop of string you can make all kinds of shapes, puzzles and games. Steve and Megumi Biddle provide all the instructions and diagrams that are needed to create their amazing string magic in another of their inventive and absorbing books.

ISBN 0 09 964470 3   £2.50

*Other great reads* from **Red Fox**

**Discover the wide range of exciting activity books from Red Fox**

## THE PAINT AND PRINT FUN BOOK
Steve and Megumi Biddle

Would you like to make a glittering bird? A colourful tiger? A stained-glass window? Or an old treasure map? Well, all you need are ordinary materials like vegetables, tinfoil, paper doilies, even your own fingers to make all kinds of amazing things—without too much mess.

Follow Steve and Megumi's step-by-step instructions and clear diagrams and you can make all kinds of professional designs—to hang on your wall or give to your friends.

ISBN 0 09 9644606   £2.50

## CRAZY KITES   Peter Eldin

This book is a terrific introduction to the art of flying kites. There are lots of easy-to-assemble, different kites to make, from the basic flat kite to the Chinese dragon and the book also gives you clear instructions on launching, flying and landing. Kite flying is fun. Help yourself to a soaring good time.

ISBN 0 09 964550 5   £2.50